THE SIREN'S CALL

DARK TIDES

BOOK FOUR

By
Candace Osmond

CANDACE OSMOND

Cover Work by Majeau Designs
Facebook.com/MajeauDesigns

DEDICATION

For Corey, whose heart and soul call to mine.

ACKNOWLEDGMENTS

As always, I have to thank my designer, Corey from Majeau Designs for putting the face and little touches on every book I do. But I also need to thank Janice Godin and Fleisha Payne for tearing through the first draft with me on such short notice. Without you guys, this book would be full of holes and probably still unfinished.

CHAPTER ONE

"Life isn't really linear. Although it's generally perceived that way. The stories we tell are woven like snakes around a divining rod. A center of time containing all that's ever been told and heard. Remembered and forgotten. Lost and found. Our pasts, presents and futures are unwound, stretched flat, cut into pieces and held up with human arms."

— Thomas Lloyd Qualls, Waking Up at Rembrandt's

What would you do if you were granted a single wish? What about three? It sounds easy enough, but it's not. It's like holding the greatest power in the whole world right in your pocket and being too scared to even think about it. I could wish for a hundred things. Save the people I love, bring back those I've lost. I could stop wars. Change the future. There were no limits to the things I could do now. I even wondered if I could wish for more enchanted pearls. But what kind of person would I become with an endless supply of demands like that? Would it corrupt my mind? Taint my soul? And then I worried that a wish like that wouldn't even work. Maybe the magic of the sirens would curse me, too, for my selfishness. Just like they did for Captain Cook and his crew on The Black Soul.

I couldn't take that chance. Not when I had so much at stake.

My feet firmly planted at the stern, I stood at my post, eyes locked on the horizon. A thin, black line that morphed and grew with the shape of civilization the closer we got. The rocky landscape slowly came into view as The Queen sailed closer to our destination and I watched as we hugged the Southern coast to Southampton. I spotted the black speck earlier that morning, but said nothing. My rational brain finally caught up with the whirlwind of emotions I'd been chasing for months and I fought with the fear of facing it all now. This was it. This was the day I'd been waiting for. I'd finally put a stop to Maria and save my mother. But something persistently ticked in the back of my mind as my fingers rolled the pearls together in my pocket.

Why hadn't I made the wish yet?

The Siren Isles were only six days away from the shores of England and my crew had spent every one of them urging me to do it. To make the wish that would lead us to Maria. But I couldn't bring myself to say the words. I wasn't sure where my hesitation came from. A little bit from every corner of my worrisome mind, I guess. I only had two wishes left and I constantly stressed over the possibility of wasting them.

Finn made it inherently clear that he thought I should wish for Maria to die. Quick and easy. But How would I really know she was dead? And what kind of closure would that be for Henry? The woman murdered his parents in cold blood, after all.

So, did I wish to find Maria myself, bring her to justice and finally rid the world of such evil? I'd save my mother in the process. But that wouldn't lead me to actually finding my mom and making sure she was safe. So, what then? Use my final wish to track down the woman who abandoned me all those years ago?

Did she even want to see me?

Nothing had forced Mom to go back in time and leave Dad alone to raise me. But, still, she left. My thoughts were constantly plagued with images and scenarios of finding her. Constance Cobham. The time traveler who started it all. I'd run toward her, but she'd be awash with anger and turn me away. And all my wishes would be gone.

"Dianna?" Henry spoke as he appeared by my side. I'd been so lost in my own mind that I hadn't even seen him climb the stairs. His concerned gaze fell on me as he neared. "Are you alright?"

My fingers released the enchanted pearls and they fell to the bottom of my pocket as I smiled. "Yes, just nervous. Eager."

He stepped closer and peered down as he reached out to tuck a straggly black curl behind my ear. "Don't be. It'll all be over soon." Henry turned and pointed at the coming horizon. "We'll reach land today."

I sighed. "I know. I've been staring at it all morning."

His hand dropped to my arm and he rubbed it comfortingly. "Still unsure about the wishes?"

I shrugged. "I'm unsure about all of it, Henry."

"How can I help?" he asked, a sense of helplessness in his tone.

I desperately searched his obsidian eyes. "Tell me what to do?" Henry sighed and pulled away. "Please, I don't know what I'm supposed to do. I don't know how...to make this right. I don't want to make a mistake."

His long thumb brushed the skin of my cheek and he leaned to press his soft lips to mine, leaving a kiss that lingered even after he gently pulled away. "Dianna, it does not matter what you wish for. I know you want to find your mother but —"

"Do I, though?"

Henry seemed confused. "How can you not? Dianna, she's your *mother*."

"Yeah, my mother who made the decision to *leave* me. To break my father's heart and shatter his soul. She left her only child with a man who ate away at himself until he was nothing more than a shell of a human being, incapable of caring for me. I've thought about it over and over...what must have been going through her mind. How she could even bring herself to consider it. I look down at my growing belly and the baby I carry inside...I just," I shook my head in defeat. "I can't imagine a day going by without looking into my child's eyes. God, I've yet to even see them and I can already understand how that feels. It would kill me to give that up."

Henry didn't look convinced. "Not everyone gets a second chance like you've been granted. Some would give anything to see their mother again. Regardless of what may have happened in the past."

My heart plummeted to the depths of my stomach. Henry's mother. He'd loved her so much and she was so brutally taken from him...by the very woman I was too scared to find. If I didn't track down Maria for myself, I at least had to do it for Henry. "I'm sorry," I told him and pressed my body to his, letting the golden scruff of his face rub against my forehead. "I didn't even consider —"

"You never need to apologize to me," he assured quietly. "I will support any decision you choose to make. I'm just trying to help you see clearly."

His strong arms wrapped around my back and hugged me tightly. The comfort and safety Henry's body provided was everything I could ever need in this world. We'd been through so much in so little time, our lives had become permanently welded together. Like two pieces of metal in the void of space, colliding and fusing together, whether they wanted to or not.

But, the more I thought about it, the more I realized that our lives had always been connected. Through my mother. There was an invisible thread that linked us; from me to my mother and, unfortunately, through Maria. In a morbid sense, our tortured pasts are what brought us together and for that I would be internally grateful.

We stayed like that for a while, silent and wrapped in one another's arms as our ship quietly sailed along the coast of England. I didn't pry my head from Henry's comforting chest until I heard the inevitable stomping of heavy leather boots making their way up the stairs.

"Captain," Finn greeted happily. His grin spread far and wide across his bearded face. "Be a matter of minutes before we begin to turn and head to port. I'd get ready if I was ye."

My heart fluttered at the thought of stepping onto land. Real land. Not just some cursed heap of sand in the middle of the Atlantic Ocean. "Thank you, Finn," I told him. "Ready the ship. Tell the others."

The eager Scot looked to Henry then and raised an eyebrow. "Have ye given thought to where we be restin' our pretty li'l heads tonight?"

Henry cleared his throat and stood taller. "I'm sure we can manage to find a local tavern with adequate lodgings."

"Aye," Finn replied thoughtfully. "Er, our treasure. Best be takin' it with us. Been too long since we stepped foot in Wallace's port. I wouldn't chance leavin' it all aboard."

Henry nodded curtly. "Yes, you're right. We shall have to pay a visit at some point, but not yet. You ready the crew. Dianna and I shall secure the loot."

Finn nodded and bound back down the stairs like a happy child. I turned to Henry. "Who's Wallace?"

"An old friend," he replied, his face void of expression. "The dealer who runs the port. All pirates who dock there must report to Wallace and pay a duty."

"A duty? For what?"

Henry sighed and shrugged, as if the matter were simple. But his shoulders carried a strange heaviness to them. "For many things. Protection from the authorities, from other pirates. Wallace also has ways of selling cargo that otherwise couldn't be sold." He tipped his head in my direction and cocked a prodding eyebrow.

It took a second, but I realized what he meant. "Ah, *stolen* goods. Wallace can sell stolen goods for pirates?"

Henry only nodded and stared out at the turning bow.

I chewed at my bottom lip. "Is that...is Wallace bad news or something? You don't seem too happy about having to see —"

"It's just been a while," Henry told me. "Being back here, it's..." he inhaled deeply and gripped the edge of the railing. "I was a different man the last time I stepped foot on English soil."

My hand slid over the hard muscles of his arm and I leaned in to place a kiss to his cheek. "That was a long time ago, Henry. People change. You just happened to change for the better." He gave me a pained smile and I squeezed his arm tighter. "You *did*."

His body twisted toward me as he slipped a steady hand across my cheek, pulling my face to his in a desperate motion. "I know," Henry said in a whisper before pressing his lips against mine. "I just need you to keep reminding me."

Our eyes locked and I could see the wet film over his reflecting the ocean's sparkling waves back to me. Like blackened mirrors, hiding his pain. "I will. I always will."

***

I stared at the full-length mirror that stood in my quarters and admired the bulbous shape of my belly, running my gentle hand over its perfect curve. I took comfort in the fact that, as long as it was inside of me, I could protect it. My precious baby. Part of me couldn't wait to hold them in my arms, but another part of my rational brain wished it would stay inside of me forever, where it could never be exposed to the harsh realities we faced every day. A pirate's life is grand, but it can be over in the blink of an eye.

Or the swipe of a sword.

The abrupt sound of knocking at my door pulled me from my worrisome mind and I turned around to find Lottie poking her head inside.

"Are you decent?" she asked.

I laughed. "Yes, come in."

The door opened all the way and she stepped inside, tall and blonde, clad in her brown leather corset that fastened tight over a long cream-colored dress. She held up a hammer in one hand and a wide, thin board in another. "I'm here to help with your trunk. Henry sent me."

"Oh, yeah, it's over there," I replied and walked with her over to my bed where my trunk sat opened next to a pile of neatly folded clothes. We peered inside and then looked to each other with a grin. I lined the base with my share of the treasure, ready to be hidden with the false bottom Lottie brought with her. The idea came to me earlier after Finn suggested we hide our treasure.

"This is brilliant," Lottie told me as she carefully lowered the board down into the trunk.

I grabbed the nails from my friend's hand and held them out for her as she hammered them in one by one. "I figured we could use one less thing to worry about on this trip. Can't leave our treasure aboard the ship, and we can't exactly leave it out in the open at a tavern or anything. We worked too hard to get it."

Lottie finished and looked to me with a proud smile. "Don't stress too much, Dianna," she insisted and touched her fingertips to my belly. "We have everything on our side."

"You mean we have the wishes on our side."

Lottie recoiled and looked away. "I didn't mean it like that –"

"Yes, you did," I said. "I know what you're all thinking and saying when I'm not around. Why haven't I made the wish yet, right?"

Lottie's fingers fiddled with the hammer in her hands. "Well," her apologetic blue eyes found mine and she shrugged, "why haven't you?"

I began packing my clothes into the trunk. "What if I make a mistake?"

"A mistake? It's a wish, Dianna, how could you possibly do it wrong? Just ask to find Maria." She handed me the pile of clothes closest to her.

"And what if Maria isn't here? What if she's nowhere near England? What then? Would a wish like that teleport us to some unknown place? Would it backfire on us?" I swallowed hard against my dry throat. "What if she's already dead? Would that kill me, too?"

Lottie's brow furrowed in thought. "Are these truly the things you worry about?"

I shrugged. "Among other stuff."

"Have you considered making sure that Maria never be able to locate your mother?"

I guffawed. "You mean drive an already mentally unstable person further into insanity?"

Lottie pursed her lips in thought. "Have you given another thought to what Finn suggested?"

I looked at her incredulously. "You mean wish my sister dead? What kind of person would that make me, Lottie? No better than her."

"Alright," my friend replied thoughtfully and sat on the edge of my bed. "Why don't we think of a different request, then? One that would ensure the outcome we want. Instead of focusing on Maria, why not wish to find your mother?"

I shook my head. "Already considered it."

"And what are your reasons against it?"

"Finding my mother will surely save her, yeah. I could warn her, she could hide." I took in a deep breath.

11

"But Maria would still be free to wreak havoc everywhere she went." Mindlessly, I continued to pack my trunk full of stuff, wandering around the room to pluck things from every surface.

"What is the true reason you won't make that wish?"

I stopped in my tracks, arms full of books and clothing. "What do you mean?"

Lottie tilted her head to the side and the corner of her mouth turned down in a disappointing frown. I let out the deep intake of air I'd been holding in and let the items I held in my arms slide into the trunk. My fingers gripped the edges of the box and my words crept from my mouth in a whisper.

"What if...what if she doesn't want to be found?"

Lottie's hand covered mine and we gripped the edge of the trunk together. "What mother wouldn't want to find her child?"

"One that decided to leave in the first place? She could have left town, left the province...but she left me behind in another era, Lottie. I mourned her death for more than half my life. What kind of a mother would do *that*?"

My friend leaned in close and looked up at my worrisome face. "I'm sure she had a good reason, Dianna. From what you tell me, you two were close. She loved you."

I stole my hand back and closed the trunk's lid, the hard sound piercing the air of my room. "People change."

"Alright," Lottie offered in defeat, "I get it." She watched as I paced around, fastening my belt and slipping on my red jacket. "Shall I suggest a third choice?"

"Knock yourself out," I replied. She narrowed her eyes. "Sorry, I mean, go ahead. I'm listening."

She let out an irritated moan. "Remember what we talked about? You must watch what you say once we arrive. You cannot let on to the fact that you're a time traveler, Dianna. They'll surely hang you for even entertaining the possibility."

My eyes rolled impatiently. "I know, I know."

She stood and crossed her arms. "I don't believe you do, not fully. Please, just...refrain from speaking as much as you can. Even I could sense there was something strange about you the moment I laid eyes on you. You wreak of otherworldliness. I can't imagine what some will think of you."

I knew she was only concerned for me, but her words still hurt. I didn't belong in this era any more than she belonged in mine. What was I doing? "I'll try my best. Now what was this other idea you had?"

"Don't rush the wish if you're unsure. Wait until we dock, and we'll spend the day sussing out the word on land, see if Maria or The Burning Ghost has been

Candace Osmond

spotted close by. If she hasn't, then we know your mother is most likely safe. Then you can decide and make your wish with confidence."

I found myself smiling, a real, true expression. "You're smarter than you give yourself credit for, you know that?"

Lottie smirked as she made her way to the door, turning back to throw me a wink before stepping outside. "I know."

CHAPTER TWO

I watched like a hungry bird as Finn and the deckhands tied us to a sturdy wharf in Southampton. The thick ropes pulled taut as The Queen swayed dockside. Gus laid the board down that connected us to the dock and I stepped eagerly onto it, struggling to keep balance with my pregnant belly. My heart raced as I neared the end, staring happily as I stuck my left foot out and touched my toes to the boards.

The ground. Firm, never moving, ground.

All around, tops of chimney stack and dull, black row of buildings cut the sky. Other boats filled the space along the docks and sailors bustled about. Throwing crates and loading goods. A swarm of smoke-stained merchant tents hugged the area next to the harbourfront. I inhaled deeply and moved ahead to let the rest of my crew off. Henry took two strides over to me and stationed himself at my side like a loyal dog. Something about the trip changed him. Changed me, even. We stepped off The Queen two very different people than the ones that stepped on back in Newfoundland. I felt wiser, stronger. But most of all, I felt that our relationship had passed some sort of cosmic test. *We* were wiser, and *we* were stronger. Together. I caught his gaze and smiled, taking his hand in mine as we stood around with the crew.

"Aye, I never thought I'd say it, but 'tis bloody good to step on land," Finn exclaimed. A resounding sigh of relief made its way through our circle. "So, the plan is?"

Henry stepped in. "We're to find lodgings and rest up for the night. It's been a long journey and I reckon we all deserve some clean clothes, a fresh meal, and a good bed." His lips pursed in thought and Henry leaned further, motioning us all to listen in. "But, bear in mind, we must practice the utmost discretion in all we do. A trip to Wallace is inevitable, but we do not have time for it right now. We've got a mission. Figure out if The Burning Ghost or Maria Cobham has been spotted around."

"Once I know for sure, I'll —" I glanced around, realizing that we weren't alone. Something I wasn't used to. "Um, once I can make a confident...decision, I will." I made eyes at my crew before me and they all nodded in understanding. I turned to Seamus and John, the two young deckhands. "I'm sorry, boys, but I need you two to stay aboard The Queen while we find a place to stay. We don't want any nosey visitors poking around when we have so much to protect. I'll send for you and the trunks as soon as I can."

"I'll stay behind with them," Gus offered gallantly.

I smiled proudly at my stoic quartermaster. "Even better." I then turned to the rest of my tired and weary crew. "Now, let's find a tavern, shall we?"

Just past the merchant tents and one dirt road up from the waterfront, we spotted a row of Victorian buildings, painted dark to match the blooms of fog and smoke. Finally, we spotted a quaint tavern that hugged the end of one long row of shop fronts. I stifled a laugh at the name carved into the wooden sign which hung outside.

The Kraken's Den.

Henry caught my gaze and peered up at the swinging sign. He gave a chuckle of his own and then squeezed my hand. "Suitable, don't you think so?"

"I'd say it's the perfect place for a bunch of pirates to rest their heads for a few nights," I told him and admired the gorgeous workmanship of carved tentacles that covered the thick wooden door.

I waited as Henry heaved it open and the four of us filed in behind him; me, Finn, Lottie, and Charlie. The large inn boasted neat wooden floors that matched its walls and the exposed beams above. The air smelled of warm food and Christmastime. And, with a closer look around, I realized it must have been close to the holiday; green garland of pine boughs hung from surfaces with red ribbon.

We came to a halt in the large entryway as a hoard of gawking guests, dispersed throughout the common areas, stared at us. I realized then just how grungy we must have looked. Months at sea. No way to properly wash our clothes, or ourselves. Even Henry's all-black leather ensemble could have used a good scrub. His long blonde hair slick with grease and pulled back in a haphazard knot. The rest of us were no better; soiled cottons, dirt smeared faces. Me, too pregnant to hide. I flushed red in embarrassment and turned my gaze to the floor as Henry made his way to the front desk.

"Do you have any rooms available?" he asked the person standing there, a tall older man with a balding head and goofy smile. "At least five or six?"

The man's words seemed to dry up in his throat as he stared incredulously at the band of misfit pirates standing in his tavern. "I-I, um, sir, I don't —"

Henry moaned impatiently and stuffed a hand in his jacket pocket, pulled out a small satchel of gold coins and plunked it down on the hard, wooden desk between them. "Let me ask you again. Do you have half a dozen rooms available, good sir?"

The startled panic washed from the inn keeper's face and he happily accepted the money. "Of course!" He ducked below the desk and popped back up with a handful of keys. "I have more than enough room to accommodate you. Will there be more joining your party?"

"Yes," Henry replied. "Three more. Two of which can share a room, if need be. We don't want to impose."

The man waved at the air. "Nonsense. The Kraken's Den can provide whatever you need, Mister..." He raised his eyebrows in wait.

Henry scooped the keys up and turned them over in his hands, eyeballing the room numbers carved into each one. "You may call me Mr. White, if you please."

The sound of Henry's true name coming over his lips surprised me. I'd never heard him say it like that before, like he owned it. But then I realized, as he turned back to us and my eyes caught his telling gaze, that he'd given that name because it was one that nobody would know.

We each took our keys and Finn adjusted his thick leather belt after pocketing his. "Aye, I'll head back to the ship, let the boys know where we be. Help 'em with the trunks."

Lottie grabbed his arm before he left. "Tell Gus I'm in room seven, would you?"

Finn grinned wildly and gave her a mocking waggle of his red brow. "Oooh!"

Lottie released his arm but gave it a hard smack before turning and heading for the large staircase behind us. But I caught her hiding a smirk as she passed me by and I couldn't help but laugh.

"Finn, be careful heading back," I told him.

Henry piped in, "There should be some wagons outside for the trunks, be sure to grab one."

"Aye, Captain," he replied, seemingly to both of us, and was off.

I turned to Henry and stuck my arm through the loop he provided with his. My body relaxed as a stale breath of air heaved from my chest and I laid my head against his firm shoulder. "Can we go to bed now?"

He chortled, deep and low under his breath. "I'd kill the man who stood in my way."

We pulled ourselves up the creaky wooden staircase, stained dark just like every other wooden surface in the tavern. The Floors, the wainscoting, and the tray ceiling were all stained an ashy ebony and I soaked it all in, the old-timey beauty of the place. Henry and I came to a stop outside door number four and I waited as he inserted the key into the hole and turned the knob.

The dark wood followed us into the room, but I admired how they painted the center squares on the wainscoting a robin's egg blue. A color they attempted to match in the bedding and scalloped canopy above. Gold finished hardware on the furniture sparkled in the sunlight that shone in through the tall, narrow window. A sweet little bench nestled into its sill. It was definitely a step up from the taverns back in Newfoundland. I wondered then, if this was the way our lives would be now. The life of the rich. As nice as it was, I still couldn't see myself living it. I much preferred the simpler life. Or that of a pirate. A stinkin' rich land dweller held no appeal for me and, as I watched Henry fit right in with his startling good looks and purposeful gait, I wondered what he truly wanted. What he saw in our future.

He closed the door behind us and I heard the lock click. "Are you tired?" he asked. "Do you wish to sleep first and wash later?"

I didn't even look back at him. My pregnant, bone-weary body zombie-walked to the giant bed and I let myself fall to it. I swear, I must have fallen asleep before the fresh linens touched my skin because that's the last I remember. My mind drifted into an empty sleep, a dark void of nothingness where I happily stayed for Lord knows how long. It wasn't until the faint tangents of a lucid dream began to fill my vision, slowly, like milk mixing with water, that my brain restarted.

Being aware inside your own dreams is an odd sensation. One that gives a slight God complex because, not only are you tuned in to everything going on, you're also slightly in control of the outcome. I stood in front of a quaint saltbox house by the sea. The wooden siding painted white, bits of it chipping away from the fists of the sea. Someone was out back, hanging clean sheets on a low-hung clothesline. The bottom of the sheets nearly touched the fresh grass below. The person was a woman, that much I could see from the long black hair that blew in the wind. She turned to me and I saw her face, a beautiful heart-shaped thing with two, big brown eyes.

Mom.

She's smiling and so am I. But hers begins to fade the closer I get. My stomach dropped and tugged at my heart, but my legs won't stop. I'm still running to her and she backs away, her face now angry.

"Mom!" I call.

But she's gone.

And then so am I.

When I awoke sometime later, the sun had moved, dimming the light of the room, but had yet to set. So, I knew only a few hours had gone by. I sat up in bed and rubbed my still-tired eyes before I realized I was alone. Pulling back the heavy blankets, I whipped myself out of bed and over to the door, but it opened before my hand touched the knob.

"Oh, you're finally awake," Henry exclaimed as he entered, carrying a large pot of steaming water over to a metal bathtub and poured it in. "I thought we could get a bath before heading down for a meal."

I yawned and then smiled as I made my way over to him. "That sounds heavenly." My lips touched his in a quick hello kiss. "Did you get any sleep?"

"A little. I nodded off for a short while, after listening to you snore." I balked and slapped his arm. The corner of his mouth quirked. "I shall sleep later, tonight, when we retire to the room," Henry replied. "I wanted to get everything ready," he gestured to the tub, "and I waited for the men to return from the ship. Ensured they got back and had no trouble at the front desk."

I chewed at my bottom lip. "Oh, yes," I said when I realized. "They wouldn't have known you used your real name."

Henry's head shook gently back and forth. "No, they wouldn't." He began to remove his clothes, bit by bit. A heap of black leather strung over a chair and I stared at his beautiful body. The way the lithe muscles moved with the twisting of his limbs. The flex of the pale skin of his chest as he slipped his soiled white blouse over his head. My eyes, as they always did, flitted to the faded pink scars that covered his body like celestial signs and I connected the dots with my mind. Tried not to envision the brutality behind each one. But, my pirate king wore them like badges of honor. Never hiding them from me. Never letting the scars, both on the surface and beneath, bleed into our lives.

Not anymore.

My hands, as if with a mind of their own, went to him. Smoothing the lines of Henry's chest and gently rubbing the hard muscles of his shoulders. And, like a mirror, his hands reached for me and I felt the rough skin of his long fingers slip under the collar of my shirt, pulling it down as he pressed his lips to the exposed skin.

I threw my head back and let Henry's mouth trail along my shoulder, neck, and then gently caress my jawline. I would never grow tired of that feeling. The sensation of his soft, warm lips touching me. I reached behind and untied the knot that held his hair back and the blonde waves fell like a curtain to his shoulders. Our yearning eyes met, and I couldn't help but smile. I loved him so much. Almost too much at times. At times like this, when the emotion overwhelmed me, and I could swear my heart would explode if not contained in its cage. With a cheeky grin, Henry tugged at the strings that held my heavy cotton skirt in place and I let it drop to my feet.

"Your bath awaits, my queen," he said coyly and took my hand as he stepped toward the steaming tub.

I laughed. "A bath. A *real* bath that I can sit in a soak. God, it's been ages." Slowly, I followed Henry into the metal basin, dipping my foot in first but then yanking it out when I felt the water. "It's scorching hot!"

The scalding water didn't seem to bother Henry as I watched him ease himself down, creating a cradle with his body and motioning me to get in. "It's really not. Only for the first moment. Come," he told me and held his hand out, "get in. The water is lovely."

Trustingly, I took his hand and let him help me into the tub. It was still hot, but as I lowered my body down onto his, my bare back nestled to his chest, I relished in the heat as it soaked into my dirty skin. I leaned back, letting my head rest against the man beneath me.

"Nice, isn't it?" Henry whispered in my ear, his tickling breath sending goosebumps scouring down my body and hardening my nipples.

I could only moan in response. The water softened my tired muscles and the steam seeped into my pores, opening them up and washing them clean. We stayed like that, soaking in the warm bath and the silence our room offered. The crackling of our fireplace the only sound to be heard. Henry's able hands sensually washed my body, paying close attention to all the neglected areas and lathered me in silky soap. When he finished, he set the soap to the side and began smoothing the skin of my stomach admiringly.

"He's getting big," he spoke softly.

I craned my neck and shifted slightly so our eyes could meet. "*He*? What makes you so sure it's a boy?"

A dreamy smile spread across Henry's scruffy face and he planted a gentle kiss on my mouth. "I'm not. Just hopeful thinking."

This was new. Henry had never expressed a preference for the baby before. Suddenly, my mind wandered to thoughts of a little boy. A full head of blonde curls bouncing as I chased him through the grass. "A boy," I said, matching his dreamy tone.

Henry continued to rub my belly. "Honestly, I don't much care what we get. I consider myself lucky enough to have the chance to be a father."

My hand slid overtop of his and we cooed over the baby inside together. "Well, if it is a boy, we can just try again until we get a girl."

"My," he replied with a smirk. "If I didn't know any better, Miss Cobham, I'd say you were trying to get me into bed."

I tipped my chin up and brushed my lips against his. "Bed, bath. Does it matter which one?"

"No," Henry told me as his hand slowly crept down my leg and then found its way back up where it nestled between my thighs. "Nothing matters as long as I'm with you."

***

The water had become tepid before Henry and I pulled ourselves out of the tub. It felt good to be clean again, truly fresh and clean over every part of my body. With a warm towel wrapped around and tucked underneath my arms, I strolled over to the trunk on the bed and opened it to fetch something to wear. Each piece of clothing I held up to my nose and gave a disgruntled moan at the damp, musty smell of it all.

"I'll send our clothes out to be properly washed," Henry told me when he noticed the growing pile of discarded choices building up.

I held up a somewhat clean red, cotton skirt. It would have to do. After slipping on a shift and covering it with a white blouse, I secured the waistline of the skirt up over my protruding stomach. "God, I'm getting huge," I noted as I stole a glance in the floor length mirror next to the bed.

Henry's hands quickly found me and slid around my torso from behind, his mouth nuzzling into my neck. "You look radiant." I tried to stifle the groan that pooled in my throat before he turned me around and planted a tender kiss on my lips, his thumb brushing the flushed skin of my cheek. "You've never been more beautiful, Dianna."

"You *have* to say that," I replied like a child.

Henry laughed and pulled away but gripped his fingers with mine and headed toward the door. "I don't have to say anything," he noted and then pulled my hand to his lips before turning the knob, "but I do have to feed you. Shall we head down for supper?"

"It's kind of late," I replied. "Do you think we missed it?"

He led me down the hall and toward the mouth of the staircase. "No, it's not like back home in

Newfoundland. This is a bustling tavern that caters to the traffic of the port. We should be able to acquire a meal at any time."

Together, we descended the stairs and I was surprised to find that he was right. Suppertime had obviously passed, the sun was long gone and the dining area had been mostly cleared out. But a few guests were left standing about. Mingling at the bar and sitting around the massive stone fireplace that anchored the common area. My eyes scanned the half-empty tavern and I smiled when I realized the faces around the fire were familiar. Finn, Gus, and Lottie. Henry noticed them, too, and we strolled over together.

"I was about to come and check on ye two," Finn said with a hearty chuckle. "Make sure ye were still alive."

I felt my cheeks flush. "I suppose I was more tired than I thought."

"We all were," Lottie chimed in as she leaned forward and set her empty plate down on the large coffee table that occupied the space between them. "I was out for a couple of hours at least. I could have slept right through 'till tomorrow if this one here didn't force me to get up." She gave Gus a playful smirk from across the center.

"Yes, well," he replied and awkwardly cleared his throat, "It was for good reason."

I saw in his eager eyes that he had news and I took a pulled one of the oversized wingback chairs over to join in the circle. Henry did the same and sidled up next to me.

"Did you find out anything?" I asked Gus.

He glanced around and then leaned in close. "Yes. The Burning Ghost sailed into port about a week ago. A merchant said she stopped at their tent and traded some things. But Maria Cobham hasn't been spotted since. If the devil's here, she's keepin' quiet. Not causing no trouble or nothin'."

"Seems suspicious," Lottie added.

I looked to Henry who was unusually silent. Even for him. Just the idea that Maria Cobham, the woman who took so much from him, could possibly be anywhere around us must have been eating him up inside. I knew his desire to end her life. But I also knew the struggle he faced by deciding not to do it, to take the higher road. We'd bring her to justice.

Eventually.

"Maria's probably just searching for my mother," I said and then, after a second thought, "*our* mother, I mean. She's most likely not distracting herself with other things. Which is good, but doesn't leave much of a trail for us to follow." I chewed at my bottom lip in thought. "Gus, where is her ship now?"

He shrugged. "I'm not sure, Captain. I was told by a number of people that a group of men came and sailed it down shore in the middle of the night. But I can't confirm that."

"Ye ken who would definitely confirm that?" Finn blurted out after taking a massive swig from a pint mug. His brow raised in wait as he eyeballed Henry.

At my side, Henry stiffened and sat up straight. "No, not yet."

"What?" I asked him, and he sighed tiredly. "If someone can help us find Maria then I think it's worth a try."

"It's Wallace," he told me with reluctance in his tone. "Wallace always knows everything that happens, every boat and person that comes and goes from the port. But we can't go there just yet. Yes, it may help, but it would most definitely deter us from the mission. We simply don't have time for that if you wish to save your mother."

"Well, then," Finn cut in and slammed his mug down on the table in front of us. "There's only one thing left to do."

Four sets of eyes slowly turned and fell on me. I moaned inwardly. "The wish."

"Aye, just do it, Lassie," Finn urged. "We know Maria's been here. And she hasn't left."

Lottie gently touched my shoulder and gave a sympathetic look. She knew my worries. "Look, if you wish to find Maria and it doesn't work, then we still have Wallace as a backup plan. We can go there for help. Not all will be lost, and you will still have one remaining pearl."

Lottie always made sense to me. She could say things in such a simple way, stripping down the problem to its basic core. Making me see clearly. I nodded. "You're right. She's here. That's all I was waiting to find out." I inhaled deeply through my nose. "It's all I need. I'll use the next pearl first thing in the morning and we'll get this done so we can finally go home."

"Aye!" Finn said loudly and raised his mug of what I assumed was ale. "I'll drink to that."

"I'll go see about getting us some food," Henry told me and stood to leave, kissing the top of my head before he walked away.

"Where's the boys?" I asked, thinking of Charlie, Seamus, and John. "They must be famished."

Gus and Finn exchanged a playful glance and Finn chuckled. "Famished, yes. But for a bitta harmless trouble, I reckon. They got cleaned up and headed out hours ago."

The thought of young Charlie finally getting the chance to have some fun warmed my heart. "That's wonderful. They're good boys. They deserve some fun."

"Did you get some sleep?" Lottie asked me.

I nodded. "But I'm still tired. I think it's the baby."

"Everything alright?" She had a pained look of concern.

"Oh, yes," I assured her and glanced down at my stomach with a smile. "Making a person is just hard work, I guess. I just need a good meal."

I barely had the words out of my mouth when Henry came from behind, balancing two plates in his hands. The smell that wafted from them seeped into my nose and made my mouth fill with warm saliva. I hadn't realized just how hungry I was until that moment. The final few weeks of our journey consisted of dried goods, salted fish, and rabbit jerky. He laid a plate in my lap. A heap of Sheppard's pie and a freshly baked bun. I took the bun and ripped it in half, dipping it in the filling of the pie and scooping it into my mouth like someone who'd been starved for days. Weeks, even. It was heavenly.

"Fork?" Henry asked, and I spotted the utensil he cheekily offered.

My friends playfully laughed at my expense as I took the fork from his grasp and continued shoveling the food into my mouth. We sat like that for a while. How long? I had no idea. But it certainly felt nice to bask in the comforts of general chit-chat and good food. A sense coziness that was clearly enjoyed in any era. The fire in front of us raged on, safely contained in it stone cage. I sat back and adored my small circle of friends as I let the warmth soak into my skin and wished I could make this moment last forever.

But, of course, like any good feeling, there's always the logical brain standing by, ready to whisk it away. I had the concrete ability to make such a silly wish. I could. If I truly wanted to. But I knew that'd be a colossal waste of the rare gift that was given to me. No, I had other things to wish for. A responsibility to my crew, to my mother. Even if I never decide to actually see her. So, I sat there, smiling, lapping up my friends' laughter and cheerful voices instead of heading to bed. For the morning brought with it a promise of something unknown. Something potentially...dark.

I was going to wish to find my sister.

CHAPTER THREE

I wasn't sure what really woke me from my sleep; the thick cold sweat that suddenly covered my body or the realistic nightmare that I was constantly falling. Nothing else. No landscape, no dialogue, no other people. Just me, free falling through space and time, no destination in sight or mind. I couldn't make it stop. So, now I just laid there in bed in a sort of stunned, motionless silence as I attempted to regain my breath.

Finally, I peeled the damp sheets from my slick body and stole a glance over to Henry who's sleeping more soundly than I ever witnessed him before. Must have been the two pints of strong ale that Finn insisted he down. Nevertheless, Henry deserved to have a drink or two after the journey we had. He deserved even more than that.

So much more.

Henry should have the life he's always wanted. The one that was so barbarically taken from him. The quaint little house by the ocean, a small farm and a boat to catch fish. A place where kids could run and play. Then a thought flashed through my mind. I knew a place just like that. But it was over three hundred years in the future. I wondered then...my final wish. If tomorrow leads us to Maria before she kills our mother...I would have one pearl left. One pearl to wish for whatever I wanted. Whatever Henry wanted.

But I shook the very thought from my mind. There was no way he'd go to the future with me. He stated as much back on The Devil's Heart. It would be an unknown world to him. Plus, I had friends here. Family, even. And a responsibility as their captain. Lottie trusted me to sail her father's ship. And my crew believed I could. They've always believed I could. I owed them everything and they blindly followed me across the Atlantic for nearly four months. The least I could do was make the damn wish that would end this journey and allow us to go home. Then I smiled as the brilliant idea entered my mind, trailing in behind my last thought like a warm light. My final wish.

I'll use it to get us home.

I laid there for a while, trying to get to sleep, but the room was too hot and the thick sheen of sweat that covered me made it impossible to relax. I needed some air. I flung my legs over the side of the bed and, ever so quietly, tiptoed across the room, grabbing my grungy red pirate's coat on the way out.

The inn was silent and held a chill in the air as I crept down the stairs toward the front door. Wrapping the jacket over my shoulders and slipping my hands through, I glanced down both ends of the old English street and took off toward the water. The sounds of my footsteps, leather against stone, flapped in the air. Stark against the eerie silence around me. The feeling of walking through a civilized village without the polluting sounds of electricity flowing all around, the bustling of vehicles, or the cry of a siren...it comforted my old soul.

Small lanterns of fire led my way to the boardwalk as I bypassed the abandoned merchant tents and touched my foot to the weathered wood that lined the length of the wharf. Funny, how eager we all were to get off The Queen and spend time on land, it was the one thing I now craved. I knew the salt of the sea air would fill my lungs and wash away my stress. I sucked it in, breath after breath, while rolling the pearls around in my pocket.

Just do it, sweetheart.

The sound of my mother's voice so loudly in my ears startled me to my core. I glanced around frantically, searching for her, but Constance Cobham was nowhere to be found. I willed my heart to slow and pinched the bridge of my nose. I had to do it. I had to make the wish then and there or there'd be no hope in getting back to sleep that night.

Slowly, I pinched one of the pearls and pulled it out from the bottom of my jacket pocket. I twirled it in my fingers, admiring the way it glistened in the moonlight. It was the grey one. I clutched it tightly and walked to the wharf's edge. With one big gulp of air, I flicked the enchanted pearl into the water and watched in awe as it began to dissipate just like the black one had done. The tiny particles were nearly gone when I realized I'd yet to say the words. I panicked and opened my mouth to speak.

"I wish to –"

But the words dried up in my mouth. The sound of my mother's voice still echoed in my head and I second guessed what I truly wanted. Wish to find Maria, or wish to find my mother first?

"I...I wish to find Maria..." There. It was done. But my heart still raced with the poison of regret. The final grains of pearl slowly fizzed away, and I shouted before it was too late, "before she finds my mother!" The weight had been lifted and I breathed a huge sigh of relief. Now I just had to wait for the universe to do its duty.

I just hoped it worked.

***

Three days had passed since I made the wish. And nothing happened. Not one single thing. No sign of Maria, not even a hint of what direction to go in. I was beginning to think it didn't work, that perhaps I waited too long, and the pearl had dissolved too much before I spoke the words. What if I did it wrong altogether? The siren didn't exactly give me detailed instructions. Worse yet, I began to worry that my first wish hadn't worked. That Benjamin was still trapped aboard The Black Soul with no way home.

But I couldn't think like that. He just *had* to be free. Benjamin risked everything, even sacrificed his own brother, for the hope that I could save him. I couldn't bear the thought that I may have let him down. So, I resorted to pacing. I walked the length of The Kraken's Den every waking minute. Scanning every corner, catching the eye of every guest I crossed paths with, and desperately searched for a clue. A signal of some sort that told me what to do.

"Knock, knock," spoke Lottie as she peeked her head in the door of my room.

Henry was downstairs getting us breakfast while I got dressed. Lottie stood in the doorway, clad in a clean creamy clue skirt and thick, grey cloak with fur that hugged her neck. I smiled and motioned her to come in.

She held up a handful of trinkets. "I came to do your hair."

My eyes focused on the trinkets she held and realized they were hair clips and combs. "Do my hair?"

What's wrong with the way it is now?" I asked and gave my head a shake, letting the straggly black curls fall down around my shoulders and upper arms.

Lottie gave that sideways look she often shot me, the one that said *just listen to me, Dianna.* "Women here have a certain image to uphold. If you don't blend in, you'll be talked about. And if you're talked about then you're noticed. And perhaps by the wrong people." She came to where I stood by the floor length mirror and placed a chair behind me. "Now, have a seat."

I sat down and watched attentively at our reflections as Lottie grabbed my heap of hair in her hands, molding and twisting and braiding until it resembled that of a beautiful up-do. She stuck gorgeous combs in place, lined with pretty beads and pearls. I almost looked like a lady. Almost.

"Where did you learn to do that?" I asked, slowly turning my head back and forth in the mirror to get a better look.

She shrugged. "I pick up things here and there. Traveling all over the place with my father meant stopping in a lot of different ports, home to many cultures." She quirked a grin at me in the mirror. "I adapt quickly."

"I bet." I stood and straightened out my heavy red skirt. "So, what's with the hair? Are we going somewhere?"

"Yes," she replied. "We're getting out of here. Let's go walk around down by the merchant tents. There's also a market square further in town. It's clear that your wish isn't going to happen by just waiting around here in The Kraken's Den."

"Yes, you're right." I sighed heavily. "I'm just…part of me is almost afraid to find her, you know?" I shook my head. "Is that cowardly of me?"

Lottie regarded me thoughtfully. "No, it's not. Maria is dangerous and unhinged. She can't be trusted." My friend's hand went to my stomach. "I understand your reasons for concern." She stepped back and raised the layers of her blue dress to reveal a leather garter full of intimidating blades and grinned widely. "But, I assure you, Maria Cobham won't lay a finger on you. Not if she wishes to keep it."

I laughed. Now *that* was the Lottie I knew.

After breakfast, I left a reluctant Henry behind with the crew while Lottie and I hopped in a carriage that led us further in town. He wanted to escort us so badly, but his presence was needed more aboard The Queen. Our ship suffered more damage from the battle of the Siren Isles than we'd originally thought, and we didn't want to arise any local suspicion by hiring men to help. Nothing screams red flag like kraken guts and smashed deck boards.

The ride was bumpy and long. We probably could have walked faster. But my pregnant self couldn't handle that long of a trek. The December air was nippy, and I tightened the fur collar of my red cloak around my neck. Lottie caught it and looked at me with concern.

"Are you cold?" she asked. "You can have my cloak, too."

I stifled a slight chortle. "Please, if I can sail across the Atlantic while fighting giant squids and fight my way off a cursed ship of insane cannibalistic pirates, then I can brave a little bit of cold air."

Lottie's unamused eyebrows rose high as she regarded me from across the small carriage house. "Pardon *me*, Captain. I meant no disrespect."

I rolled my eyes, mostly at myself because that wasn't the first time my pregnancy hormones had gotten the best of me lately. "I'm sorry, I didn't mean –"

Lottie let out a loud cackle of laughter and it took me a second to realize she was messing with me. My brave, badass knife-ninja best friend so very rarely showed the carefree lighter side she held under the shadow of her usual quiet self.

"It's quite alright, Dianna. You're not the first pregnant woman I've dealt with." She peered out the little window to our left. "Don't dance around my feelings and won't dance around yours."

My lips spread far and wide. God, she was the best. "Deal." We jostled to and fro as the carriage turned a corner. "So, speaking of feelings, how are things with you and Gus?"

Her pale cheeks flushed a pleasant rose. "As fine as they could be, I suppose."

"Just *fine*?"

Her eyes rolled. I knew she hated talking about the details, but that's what friends do so I urged her with my widened eyes, but Lottie continued to scan the world outside the window. "A lady never tells."

"Well, I'm no lady," I started, egging her on. "Things between Henry and I have never been better. He's...different. Happier. And, surprisingly, the sex is still amazing considering I'm a million years pregnant."

I could see she was biting back a grin. Finally, Lottie sighed happily. "Things are...just as good with Gus and I."

We caught one another's playful gaze from the corner of both our eyes and erupted into a fit of laughter. Eventually, the giggles subsided as Lottie's face turned serious.

"Y'know, he told me about his wife," she said.

I fought back a look of surprise. Gus was clearly getting serious with her, then. "Oh? And how did that go?"

Lottie's shoulders slumped. "I'm not sure, really. I mean, I'm thankful he's opening up, willing to move on and take the next step with me. But it's odd, don't you think?"

"Odd?"

"I don't know." Her head shook quickly. "Perhaps I'm being silly. I haven't a clue what I'm doing."

"Look, that part of Gus, his past, his...the man he used to be," I began, "I'm sure he's put it all behind him now. But it's still a very big part of who he is, and I think the fact that he was comfortable enough to share that with you means something."

"You think so?"

I nodded. "He wants you to know the person he used to be, so you'll learn to love the man he's become."

Lottie's face lit up. "Like you did with Henry?"

I was taken aback by the statement. Mostly because I'd never really thought of it like that. But, in a way, I knew the person Henry used to be before I ever even met him. Through his journal. My heart cried for the poor boy in the words, and then fell in love with the man he became. His past was such a huge part of him, woven into his very soul.

And he wanted to share that with me.

"Yeah," I replied with the ghost of a smile, "I suppose so."

We sat in a comfortable silence for a few more minutes until, finally, the carriage came to a stop and the rickety door swung open to reveal the driver awaiting our exit.

"Market Square, Madams," he told us as he took my hand and helped me down the single step to the ground.

I nodded politely and stood waiting for Lottie to follow. I glanced around and absorbed the strange beauty of where we were. A long, narrow alley-like area filled with merchant tables covered with small canopies and shop fronts which lined each side. In the distance, a set of cobblestone stairs cut across the width of the stretch and led to what looked like larger shop fronts. The smells of various things; dried fish, roasting meats, baked goods, and flowers all filled my nose and competed for a place there. Ultimately, the baked goods won, and I took Lottie by the hand as I made my way over to the quaint shop which had a hand-painted sign on the window that read Samson's Bakery. Their front door was open and delicious smells of breads and cookies poured out.

I inhaled deeply. "God, that smells like home."

"Let's go in, then," she suggested. "I'm sure the boys wouldn't say no to some fresh biscuits!"

We were like two giddy children as we loaded up on delicious buns and cookies. The kind baker, a short and plump lady with grey curls that reminded me of Aunt Mary, neatly wrapped everything and handed it over in a pretty basket. We thanked her and went on our way, weaving in and out of shops, stopping to strike up casual chit-chat with people walking about. Because, even though we seemed light-footed and carefree, our mission was never far from my mind.

Find Maria.

A fact that Lottie never forgot, either, I realized as she began slipping in questions about the port and recent pirates that may have come through. We spent the better part of the morning there in the busy merchant square, asking and prodding and listening, but were still no closer. I truly began to panic at the thought of my wish not working. I only had one more left and I wanted to use it to get us home.

After I'd eaten half of the contents in my basket, we planted our defeated selves on a cold stone bench on the upper section of the square, surrounded by the larger shops that were clearly for the wealthier customers. The windows boasted bright colors of reds and blues, radiant emerald green dresses, sparkling jewelry and handbags. But one store stood out to me among the rest. An apothecary.

"Mind waiting here for a moment?" I asked Lottie and she followed my gaze.

"The apothecary?"

I shrugged. "There's a few things I'd like to get, if they have it."

She didn't look convinced. Lottie leaned back against the bench and replied, "No, I go where you go."

"Alright, then," I told her. "I just wasn't sure if you were sick of walking around." But the tired look on her face told me I was right. Then something dawned on me and I chortled. "Henry told you not to leave my side, didn't he?"

My friend failed to hide the way her cheeks flushed, her eyes flittering away from mine. "Not really," Lottie started. "I saw how torn up he was about the idea of you leaving without him, so I told Henry I wouldn't let you out of my sight. He never replied but the look on his face said, '*you better not*'. So…"

I heaved a sigh but smiled for my friend. For the way she always jumped in, ready to protect anyone. "To the apothecary we go."

Inside the old, charcoal colored store awaited an interior unlike anything I'd ever seen before, sitting in a cloud of incense and herbs. Wall to wall, ceiling to floor shelves that were completely full of jars and tiny boxes. All sorts of sizes, shapes; glass, stone. Each one labeled in a fancy scrawl. I titled my head to the side and approached the shelves closest to me, straining to read what they were. Crow's Foot. Amethyst Dust. Milk of the Poppy. No rhyme or reason to the way items were placed. Still, it was beautiful. Wondrous chaos.

"May I help you, ladies?" croaked a voice in the distance. Lottie tightened at my side as I scanned the shop for its source. My eyes landed on an elderly woman, freakishly tall and mostly bones. A strange navy-blue fabric draped itself over her narrow frame, tucking and twisting around limbs. Mesmerizing jewels and brooches pinned pieces and a gold sash kept it all together. Dry, grey curls fanned around her arms as she stepped forward, giant wooden bracelets clanking. "My name's Theodora."

"Pleased to meet you," I replied and stepped to meet her in the center of the beautiful shop. "I'm Dianna and this," I motioned to Lottie, "Is Charlotte."

Theodora lazily smiled and turned to light a flame under a tiny pot of incense. Sandalwood, by the smell of it. Like my father used to wear.

"I'm looking for some lavender, as well as some loose, dried chamomile. If you have it?" I wasn't a hundred percent sure things like that would exist in this era. But it would have been great if they did.

The old lady's eyes looked interested as her brows raised. "Having trouble sleeping, are we?"

I could feel Lottie next to me, her curiosity peaked. "Yes," I told Theodora. "I'm pregnant. Nearly five months. And it's become fairly difficult to sleep." I wanted it for myself, but also for Henry. I knew my disrupted, broken sleep kept him up all night, too. And with the stress of saving my mother on my shoulders, I found it impossible to relax enough to sleep through the night.

"A woman who knows herbs and oils," Theodora said and grinned before stepping closer. "You've had trouble sleeping before?"

"No." I stuffed my hands in the large pockets of my red skirt. "I just know those help."

"Very well, then," the woman seemed satisfied with my answer then glanced to Lottie. "Anything for you, dearie?"

Lottie waved her off as she stepped away. "No, thank you. I'll just look around."

"So," Theodora regarded me curiously, "Pregnant, are we?" I nodded. "Do you know what you're having yet?"

My face twisted in thought. "How –"

"Oh, I have many ways to tell." I watched as the kooky old woman roamed around the store, eyes scanning shelves, until her hands reach up on a shelf to pluck a small brown box, just big enough for a pair of shoes. From inside it, she pulled a long golden chain which dangled with a jagged stone. Milky white, like marble. "Do not be alarmed. 'Tis no witchcraft."

"What are you going to do?"

"Just hang it over your stomach like so." She held the chain up high and the stone hovered just a few inches from the surface of my belly. Quietly, she waited until it was perfectly still. Suddenly, the pale rock began to gently sway back and forth, and I lit up with curiosity. "When the pendulum swings side to side, it's a boy. But when it begins to move in a circle –" she paused and grinned as the stone started to change its motion. "It's a girl."

I didn't really believe in that sort of stuff. Or so I thought. But when Theodora spoke the words, my mind filled with bright colors of pink and purple. Of long, blonde curls bouncing around as she went through life. A girl. *My* girl. "Well," I replied, "that would be wonderful."

"Now, let's get you your things, shall we?" Her long boney fingers curled around my arm after she pat it once, leading me with her. "Now, the dried chamomile. I assume it's for drinking? For tea?"

"Yes," I confirmed. "I'll need something to steep it with, as well."

Theodora let go of my arm and climbed up the first two steps of a thick, wooden ladder. "The thing about pure chamomile is that it's too potent. You must mix it with something." She scanned the shelf in front of her pointed nose and pulled out a large stone jar. "White tea. From the Caribbean. Just a mild, loose tea and, when mixed with chamomile, will lull you into a warm, comfortable sleep."

"I'll take it," I told her. "Thank you."

Her stick-like legs lowered her to the floor and she set the jar on a butcher block top before strolling over to another set of shelves, this one with wiry racks of tiny vials. "And lavender. It's also pure and strong. Only use a dab here or there. A little behind the ear or rub on a pillow." Her eyebrows raised in wait as she urged me to acknowledge.

"Yes, of course. I'll be sure to remember that." I craned my neck to find Lottie who was circling the store, mindlessly searching through the contents on shelves and tables.

"You know, sometimes changing the room in which we sleep can help with restlessness." Theodora's thin fingers gently opened jars and poured oils, mixing and wrapping, packing my ingredients in smaller vessels. "Blocking out any light from a window, making the bed more suitable. Those kinds of things."

"Thanks, but I'm staying at a tavern, so the sleeping conditions are what they are," I told her reluctantly.

"Oh? A visitor, then? What fine establishment are you staying with?"

"The Kraken's Den. Near the docks. My crew and I pulled in just a couple of days ago." I noticed Lottie come back within sight, stepping to my side with a curious stance.

She gently grabbed my arm and pulled me off to the side. "Do not tell anyone where we are staying, Dianna," she whispered loudly.

I was about to protest. I hadn't really given up any dire information. But then I gave it a second thought. That Wallace guy. Henry had said every pirate who pulls into port was expected to report to Wallace and pay a duty. We'd been avoiding the trip because Henry claimed we didn't have time for the distraction. I began to wonder then, what sort of distraction it would really cause. I shrugged it off. There's no way the old-world pharmacist could tell that we were pirates. We were dressed like upstanding ladies. But, one look at Theodora, the sudden appearance of a sly grin across her wrinkled face, told me that she'd been prying for information.

I gave her a look of disappointment but said nothing other than, "How much for the goods?"

After we paid, I walked out of the shop with a heavy cloud over my head. Henry seemed concerned with avoiding Wallace and I'd never really asked why. Not for details, anyway. But I couldn't help but feel that I'd done something seriously wrong back there. The repercussions of which I didn't even know.

"Do you think I said too much?" I asked Lottie as we walked side by side down the wide cobblestone alley toward the smaller shops and merchant tents.

She seemed to ponder on it for a moment. "No, I'm sure it's fine. I just had a bad feeling about that woman."

"Theodora?" I confirmed, and then stopped as something in one of closer tents caught my eye. "Yeah, I know what you mean."

I broke free of our stride and headed for the long, wooden counter. Its surface was covered in rustic trays of mismatched items. Brooches, rings, books, small weapons. A hand-painted sign read *POST*. A trading post! Like an old-school pawn shop. But of all the fantastical trinkets, only one really caught my eye. My trembling hand reached out a plucked a ring from its display. A golden band with an emerald nestled in a claw.

Henry's mother's wedding ring.

My breath caught in my throat as I turned the piece of jewelry over in my hands, examining and making sure it truly was the long-lost treasure. It was. I'd know it a mile away. Tears welled in my eyes and I looked to the merchant. "Where did you get this?"

The man, aged and weathered, took stock of the item I held. "That?" he started, "Someone came through last week and traded it." He moaned as he leaned down behind the counter and lifted a small wooden crate. "That and everything in here."

I peered in and a gasp escaped my throat. A ship-in-a-bottle, a black leather journal, a compass, and other things. Henry's things. My free hand reached in and scooped up the model ship, noting the inscription. H.W.W. My blood began to boil with anger. These were all aboard The Devil's Heart when it sunk to the bottom of the harbor.

"Who brought you these things?" I demanded angrily. Lottie was by my side then.

The old merchant appeared panicked. "I-I am not sure, Miss," he stammered.

"Yes, you do!" I yelled and grabbed the small crate, clutching it to my chest, the tears slowly escaping and dribbling down my one cheek. These were the only things left from my first home in 1707 before it was savagely burned and sunk to the bottom of Harbour Grace. "You said they came through just last week."

"What's going on?" Lottie asked me.

"This stuff," I muttered, still angry. "It's Henry's! All of it. From The Devil's Heart."

My emotions were bubbling over and it was all I could do to contain them. I knew scavengers went to the site where it sank, but seeing these things brought back some memories. Both good and bad. Flashes of images danced through my mind; getting yanked from the sea, being locked in the storage hold, the gunshot and the cook. Then my mind went to Henry and how I slowly peeled back the layers and fell in love with the man I found. My time on The Devil's Heart was a rollercoaster of events and it brought me to him. It's where everything started. But what were the chances the belongings would end up there? In a place where I was looking for my sister. It had to have been her.

Lottie plucked a dagger from her hidden garter and discreetly held it out, pointed toward the man. Her face twisted with sheer intimidation. "Tell me who gave this to you or I'll take you out back and gut you from your nose down."

The merchant's eyes widened in horror and he held up in his hands in defeat. "Look, I do not wish for any trouble. Please —"

I leaned in with an urgent whisper, "Was it Maria Cobham? Did the woman look like me? Just older?" I asked him desperately, almost afraid of the answer I already knew. He only nodded.

I looked at Lottie and she regarded me from the side. "See? I told you."

I bit back the rest of my tears and pulled myself together. "Do you know where she went? Where she is now?" The poor man seemed frazzled and helpless. I knew he had no further information. But, surely, this was a sign of some kind. A connection. My wish finally unfolding and pulling me in the direction to find my insane sibling. "I'll buy this crate from you," I told the merchant and his shoulders sank with relief.

Lottie leaned over the table, dagger still pointed in a threatening direction. "But if Maria comes through again, or you hear of her whereabouts, you must let us know." With her empty hand, she reached into the satchel she wore and pulled out a tiny bag of coins. Discretely, she shoved it toward the man. "I trust you'll remain quiet about everything. Come and find a man named Gus at The Kraken's Den if you have anything worth sharing."

The merchant accepted the bag of schillings and nodded purposefully. "I swear to it."

Lottie sneered and backed away, returning her weapon to its hilt under the thick layers of her dress. "Good."

I loosened the string of my red leather coin bag, ready to pay the man whatever he wanted for Henry's belongings, but he held his hands out to stop me. "No, no, please," he said. "Just take them."

"Are you sure?" I asked, hesitant of his reasoning.

He gave me a nervous smile and tilted his head, hands open. "I have no need for them. And they clearly mean something to you. Please," he urged, "Take them. I insist. Consider it a gesture of good faith."

"Well, I at least want to pay for the ring," I told him as I plucked a few gold coins from my pouch and placed them on the table between us. More than enough, I was sure. He would have sold it to someone, made money. He was running a business, after all. And I respected that.

The merchant's eyes flicked to Lottie by my side, almost as if he awaited her approval. When she didn't react, he finally gave a nod and slipped the coins into his pocket. "If you must."

"I do," I replied and swiped an empty red velvet sack from the table. "I'll take this as well."

We bid him farewell and made our way down through the bustling merchant square toward our awaiting carriage. I'd transferred the contents of the crate and the other items I purchased to the more convenient drawstring sack and held it tight to my chest, arms wrapped around it as if it held the most precious things in the world. And, in a way, it did.

Henry's journal, his past contained in its pages, in his mother's blood. The ship-in-a-bottle I gave to him as a present, after the first night we made love. And his mother's emerald ring. The one thing he so desperately wanted me to have on our wedding day. Henry was heartbroken over its loss. He never really said as much, but I could tell. Now, as we approached the carriage, I imagined the look on his face when I showed it to him. My heart warmed.

"You know," I said to Lottie, "You probably didn't need to threaten that man back there. I'm sure he would have been fine with payment. Money talks."

She laughed as our driver opened the door for us to step in. "As does a blade. And it's a conversation he won't forget. I had to make sure he would do as I asked."

She went in first and I handed her the heavy bag as I followed behind, unable to stifle my own laughter. It's like she had no idea the power she held just by being a woman. "I'm sure he would have listened to you, regardless."

"What do you mean?"

We took our seats and settled in for the long, bumpy ride. "Lottie, you're drop dead gorgeous. I'm sure you could make any man do whatever you wanted."

Her face crumpled in disgust. "I'd rather die than lower myself to those standards. My beauty is not a weapon. If anything, it's a curse. I've had to become much stronger than one should ever be in order to deal with the people who've tried to use my appearance to their advantage."

I stared at her admiringly. My friend was a wonder. A rare gem, that was for sure. "And that's why I love you, Charlotte Roberts." I chuckled. "You're such a badass."

I caught a glimpse of her blue eyes rolling at my expense as she glanced out the tiny carriage window. "I'm not sure what that means." I sat and awaited her usual lecture about my modern tongue. Instead, she regarded me with a pleasant grin. "But, I quite like it."

We spent the whole ride immersed in a conversation about strong females from my time and how far women will come. Lottie was mesmerized by my words, my affirmations of our future as a gender. I told her of the hurdles women will eventually face, the sexism that still lingers in the threads of modern day. She seemed fascinated by suffrage and admired how woman persisted. I could picture Lottie fitting in quite well in the future. Fighting for women's rights. Owning her sexuality as she should. She reminded me of an old-world Jessica Jones or Sarah Connors. Only she wasn't a superhero. She was real, and I felt beyond lucky to call her my friend.

Finally, we pulled to a stop and the door flung open once again. The driver stood loyally, waiting to help us step down to the ground below. It felt weird being carted around and aided to and from a vehicle. I almost felt like someone important.

Lottie handed me the velvet sack before her hand reached out and hauled on the thick, tentacle carved wooden door of The Kraken's Den. As soon as we entered my eyes scanned the common areas and I felt my heart flutter wildly as they landed on a small trio of men standing around the stone fireplace in the back. One of which was Henry who turned and caught my eager gaze. We both smiled and casually strolled to one another. Heart reaching for heart.

"I missed you," he whispered deep and raspy against my ear. His lips found mine and I succumbed to the smell of leather and red wine, the way the blonde scruff of his face gently scratched against the skin around my mouth. Finally, he pulled away, leaving me breathless.

Damn, he knew how to kiss a girl hello.

Head swimming, I smiled and kidded, "I believe you." I so desperately wanted to show him the treasure I'd found. But alone. Upstairs where Henry could have the space to deal with his emotions freely without the audience of our crew and the guests of the Den. "How's the ship?"

"In better shape that we thought," he told me. "We should be finished tomorrow."

"Good, I want everything to be ready for us." I rubbed my lips together in nervous thought. "I want to leave the second this is over."

"Oh, you shan't be leavin' any time soon," spoke an unknown voice from over my shoulder.

I witnessed the color drain from Henry's face and his charcoal eyes widen as Finn and Gus flanked his sides, hands on their weapons. Slowly, I spun around, Henry's hand tight around my wrist. Two men stood there; big, burly, and most definitely intimidating. I hadn't seen them there at the tavern before. They must have followed us in; a confirmed suspicion as one of the men grabbed Lottie from behind his back and pushed her forward where she fell into Gus's arms.

"Excuse me?" I asked while attempting my toughest face, clutching my sack behind me.

"Dianna," Henry whispered with urgency. "Don't –"

The man, tall and broad with greasy dark hair that stuck out from underneath a flat cap, stuck a hand out to shake in mock politeness. "Forgive me, my name is Frank. You'll be comin' with us, now." Frank watched me blatantly ignore his gesture and his hand dropped back to his side with a sneer.

"Me?" I clarified. Henry's grip around my wrist tightened and he pulled me back, closer to him.

"Yes," the man named Frank replied. "You, and your crew. The lot of ya."

"I don't even know you," I said to him. "I demand to know where it is you expect me to go."

Frank's eyes bypassed me, and he failed to stifle a knowing smile as he scanned around the room, taking in the faces of my crew as if he knew them. "Why don't you ask them? They surely know." He paused and locked his threatening gaze on Henry over my shoulder. "Don't you, Captain Barrett?"

Those annoying little hairs stood up on end as goosebumps scoured over my body. *Captain Barrett*? I turned and pulled my arm back, my hand falling into his and staying there as Henry refused to let me go.

"Henry?" His name carried with it the tone of my confusion. He looked...almost apologetic. "What is he talking about? Where are we going?"

Henry's tongue flicked out and moistened his dry, nervous lips. His expression held a depth of explanation, but he only spoke three curt words. "To see Wallace."

CHAPTER FOUR

I sat across from Lottie and Gus as I rubbed my arm where Frank had hustled me into their carriage. The horse had trotted off before Henry could jump in and I barked at the driver to stop. But he ignored my demands. I hadn't had a chance to stow away my velvet satchel of treasures before Wallace's men scooped us up, so I wrapped the thick drawstring around my hand, ensuring no one would take it from me. The items inside may not mean much to an outsider, but they were everything to me. To Henry. I at least wanted the chance to give them to him.

I also wanted the chance to talk to him about this Wallace guy. How should I act? What should I say? Not say? I hadn't the faintest idea of what we were being led to and my expectations of a good outcome were low. That much I got from the solemn looks on my carriage mate's faces.

"Okay," I finally said to them. "What's going to happen?" Lottie said nothing as she chewed her lip in worried thought. "Gus?" I asked desperately. "Are we in trouble? Danger? What do I do?"

He regarded Lottie from the side and leaned forward on his lap, motioning me to draw closer. "Wallace runs the port," he began and crinkled his brow. "The pirate portion of it, anyway. No one comes or goes without payin' a visit to Wallace first. They must offer their duty for protection from the crown."

My stomach tightened. "So, Wallace thinks we were avoiding paying our fee?" Gus nodded. "What happens to those who don't pay?"

Gus shrugged nervously. "Nothin' direct. Wallace makes damn sure no trail leads back. But I've seen ships burned, men's throats slit in the night, the authorities called. It's been years since Henry and I've been back here, but I reckon it's all the same."

My trembling hands wrung together. "So, what do I do, then? How do I act? What do I say?"

"You speak of nothing," Gus replied.

"But she's the captain," Lottie retorted, pulling the combs from her hair and letting it fall loose around her shoulders.

Gus's furrowed brow regarded me with pity. "Not to Wallace, she ain't." He inhaled deeply, ready to continue, but Lottie slid from her seat and gawked out the tiny carriage window in awe, gasping at the sight.

"My God," she exclaimed. "I'd never been here before, father always left me behind on The Queen when we docked in Southampton. Said Wallace's was no place for a child." She chortled. "It was the only time he ever referred to me as one." Her eyes stared out the window in amazement. "Just look at this place."

I shifted across my seat and joined her admiring gaze. The two carriages bumped along a well-groomed dirt road that wound through a gorgeous property, the sides of our path lined with flowering fruit trees. In the distance, at the end of the ridiculously long tree-lined road, stood a magnificent white house. No, it was far too large for a simple house. The closer we got the more it came into view, its impressive size filling my entire line of sight. Endless rows of windows and peaks overwhelmed my brain.

Our carriage neared the front entrance, a gaudy set of navy-blue doors with gold embellishments, and we circled around a stone fountain before we came to a final stop. Gus kicked the door open and helped Lottie and I to the ground. My neck craned as my eyes hungrily took in the sight in its entirety. The property was like something out of an old Victorian painting. A massive home fit for a king with a backdrop of the wide-open sea behind it. I realized then, the property sat on a cliff, backed by the serene soundtrack of the tumbling waves below.

The second carriage came up right behind us and Henry jumped out before it came to a full stop. He took two long and quick strides to me, his arms embracing my body protectively. To my ear his face nuzzled and whispered desperately, "Say nothing. Do not let on that you are the captain. The repercussions will be much different if Wallace discovers who truly sails The Queen."

I pulled away and searched his worried eyes. "But, Henry –"

"No," he barked quietly. "I will not put that on you. For today, I am the captain." He saw my unwillingness to play the damsel. "Dianna, *please*."

My lips pursed in thought as I fought back my pride. "Fine."

Henry visibly relaxed and opened his mouth to speak again but was interrupted by an approaching Finn.

"Aye, Captain," Finn said to me, "Are ye alright?"

I gave him a quick nod and then replied, voice lowered, "Here, I'm just Dianna. Henry is the captain, okay?"

"It's for her protection," Henry added.

Finn seemed about to protest, but Henry grasped his shoulder, stressing the importance of the matter. After a moment, Finn nodded dutifully. "As you wish, Dianna." He chuckled. "Christ, that feels strange on the tongue."

I couldn't help but smile. "I promise, if we get through this, you can go back to calling me whatever you want."

Lottie and Gus joined us as we stood and waited outside the gargantuan property and part of me thanked the heavens that Charlie and the boys weren't there. It was then that I noticed a wooden sign, swinging in the wind on its cast iron stand near the front door. It appeared to be hand carved and distressed over time, the words etched into its surface telling me that it was more than just a house. I squinted to read what it said.

The Siren's Call.

I peered up at Henry, his hand clasped tightly around mine. "Is this a fancy tavern or something?"

"Of sorts," he replied vaguely.

"What does that mean?"

"Once upon a time, when it belonged to Wallace's father, The Siren's Call was a place for people of stature and title to stay under the protection and discretion it offered," Henry explained.

Finn must have noted my look of confusion because he leaned over and whispered from the side of his mouth, "'Tis a brothel for kings and rich bastards."

At my side, Henry stiffened. "But that all ended when Wallace inherited the property and business."

I found that fact strange. The amount of money men like that would pay would surely be a lucrative business. "Why's that?"

The men who'd scooped us from The Kraken's Den strolled up to the front doors and gripped the golden handles before hauling them open. I stood with my crew in wait as two more men exited the house and stepped off to the sides as someone emerged from between them. A silent gasp escaped my lips. The person exuded confidence with a chin held high and creamy brown skin as radiant as melted milk chocolate. As I took in the shocking beauty of their heart-shaped face framed with long, shiny black waves, I realized why Wallace didn't want The Siren's Call to be a brothel. I suddenly knew why Henry and my crew always seemed uneased at the mention of Wallace's name.

Because Wallace was a woman.

The tall, dark beauty gave a curt nod to her men as she graced the few steps that led down to the ground where we stood. Her lithe body wrapped tightly with a brown leather corset, arms bathed in a flowing white silk, she was almost painful to look at. I suddenly felt like the grungy, bloated pregnant woman I was, and my cheeks flushed red as she neared.

"Gentlemen," she addressed the group and then Lottie, "and lady. I see many familiar faces." Her dark brown eyes then fell on me and she approached like a cat stalking a mouse. "But yours I do not recognize. Tell me why."

"Roselyn," Henry cut in and she regarded him with widened eyes. He cleared his throat. "Wallace, may I present to you my fiancé, Dianna...Sheppard."

My father's last name. I noted how Henry hid the fact that I was a Cobham. Roselyn Wallace must have known Maria. But I began to worry...if she knew my sister then, surely, my appearance might seem suspicious. I silently begged for her not to see the resemblance.

"Fiancé, you say?" Her big, brown eyes flickered to my belly and then back to Henry. "And with child? My, you've been busy, Captain Barrett."

"Yes," Henry replied. "A lot has changed since I last left these shores."

Wallace said nothing, only wavered in front of us thoughtfully before turning on her leathered heel. I couldn't figure out her expression; a mixture of surprise and...jealousy? No. It couldn't be. What would this woman have to envy over me? But my heart clenched in my chest as a thought ran through my mind.

Was it possible that she and Henry were together in the past?

If so, why wouldn't he have told me? I guffawed internally. Heck, why hadn't he told me Wallace was woman? Suddenly, things made more sense. Recent conversations turning vague and deflecting each time the topic of Wallace was brought up. I watched as Henry's eyes followed the dark beauty away from us and my paranoia began to set in. Were those looks of longing? Regret? Something else? I didn't want to think such things but the pit in my stomach turned sour and my mind swam in circles. The ground rose toward my suddenly sweaty face.

I was passing out.

The strong bars of Henry's arms dug into my body as he caught me and held me close. "Christ, Dianna! Are you alright?" My head still spun with cloudy swirls, but I managed a nod as my vision turned black. Henry moaned disapprovingly. "No, you're most certainly not."

I felt Lottie's cool hands on my face. "Dianna, what's the matter? What happened?"

"Christ, she's as white as a bloody ghost," Finn threw in. "We best be gettin' her back to the tavern."

"N-no," I whispered tremblingly. "I'm fine. I just...I haven't eaten in a while." A big fat lie. Lottie and I had stuffed our faces at the market. But I didn't really know what was wrong. Overwhelming emotions, yes, but that shouldn't have caused me to faint.

"Is she alright?" I heard Wallace ask, surprised by the string of sincerity in her voice. Maybe I had pegged her wrong. "Come, get her inside. We can talk business in there." I heard the crunching of the woman's footsteps as she strut toward the house and snap her fingers. "Angus bring the carriages around back and have the horses tended to."

"Yes, ma'am," the man named Angus replied dutifully.

Henry's arms shifted as he hoisted me into his grasp, cradling me tight to his strong chest while he carried me inside with ease. It was all I could do to wrap my own arms around his neck. My heavy head lulled back, my neck unable to support it. Through the cloudy tunnel vision, I caught glimpses of The Siren's Call; elaborate paintings as large and gaudy as the house itself, perfect Victorian furniture displaying delicate vases and sculptures. The floors were some sort of stone. White like marble, from what I could tell. And the sound of footsteps rang loud through the halls. Finally, we turned a corner and entered a large, brightly lit room.

"Set her over there on the chaise," Wallace instructed as she stood in front of a wall of bookcases. "I'll have Ansley fetch her some water and a bite to eat."

Henry gently laid my limp body down on a velvety surface and I immediately began to feel better. The blanket of nausea slowly melting away. With great difficulty, I tried to sit up.

69

"No, no," Henry told me. "Lay down."

I waved his hand away. "I'm fine, really," I insisted stubbornly and shifted my back to rest against the arm of the chaise. "I'm starting to feel better."

I must have looked it because Henry allowed me to remain sitting up. But he took a seat right by my side. "Are you sure?" I nodded and gave a shaky smile. His hand cupped my cheek as his thumb caressed the skin under my eye. "What happened back there?"

I shrugged. "I think...perhaps I overdid it today? With the walking and –" I searched around me in a panic. My satchel. It was gone.

"Here," Lottie said and stepped closer before handing me the bag. "You dropped it outside."

I gave her an appreciative smile as I felt my shoulders relax and I eased back. "Thank you."

"Is it the baby?" she asked with concern.

"No, I don't think so." I fumbled nervously with the drawstring, wrapping it around my hand. "Like I said, I think I just...the exhaustion of the day caught up with me. That's all."

My friends still remained unconvinced, that much I could tell by their lingering looks of concern. Thankfully, I was saved from endless prying as Roselyn Wallace came back into the room, carrying with her a shiny metal tray. We all stopped and watched as she set it on a thick, gaudy desk of darkened wood. The woman grabbed a cup of something steaming and came toward me.

"Here, she said, holding out the cup. "Some warm broth from Ansley's soup. Drink it. You'll feel better."

I looked to Henry and he gave a faint nod, so I accepted the cup of soup with a smile.

"Uh, thanks." I gently placed the rim to my lips and inhaled the surprisingly delicious aroma. Definitely some sort of chicken-like meat and veggies, from what I could smell. The broth was a creamy brown, inviting me to drink up. I did. The delightful taste, and almost immediate feeling of nausea passing, tempted me to drink more and more until the large ceramic cup was empty.

Roselyn smiled, a gesture that didn't quite reach her eyes. "Excellent." She walked around the backside of her oversized desk. "Now, let's talk business."

Henry stepped forward. "Wallace, let me –"

"Captain Barrett." She glared toward him. "I will do the talking and asking of questions. I've played nice long enough. I watched your ship sail into port. I saw your mismatched crew step off and head to town. For days, I waited. Expecting that you'd come see me once you'd settled in." Her hand reached out and grabbed a small dagger from the surface of the desk, toyed with it in her hand. "After all, if the rumors about your crew ring true, you'd owe me quite the duty. I'd hate to think you were planning on leaving without paying it."

"And what rumors would that be, exactly?" Henry crossed him arms sternly over his chest.

Wallace narrowed her eyes and grinned, pointing the tiny dagger around the room, it's tip hovering in front of each one of my crew. "A little birdie told me you paid a visit to Shell Bird Island. The *real* one."

"And what of it?" my pirate king asked.

"We all know of Peter Easton's treasure, the one said to have been hidden at Shell Bird Island down in Newfoundland. Many a man have traveled in search of it. I admit, even I've sent a crew or two down. But no one's ever been able to find it." Her voice lowered. "But I'm betting you did." She walked back and forth, dragging the dagger across the desk. "Didn't you?"

A tight silence held the room, moments passing before anyone spoke. Finally, Henry let out an impatient sigh. "No, we didn't."

Wallace's eyes bulged as her long legs swiveled in front of the desk and advanced on our group. "Lies!"

Finn and Henry pushed at the space between them and Wallace. Henry's nostrils flared in anger. "Watch it, *Roselyn*."

She shot him a glare, but he refused to correct himself. A wide range of expressions and emotions passed between the two but neither backed down. Finally, unable to take the tension in the room, I opened my mouth and blurted out whatever came to mind.

"We found the damn island!" I shouted. My crew seethed in my direction. But Wallace only smirked. "We had the treasure. But our ship caught a massive storm on the way here. We lost everything and just about ourselves, too. That's why the ship has been in repair."

"'Tis true, Wallace," Finn added as he rolled back on his heels and adjusted the heavy leather belt around his waist.

"Finnigan Artair." Wallace turned her attention to the giant Scot in the room. "It's good to see you alive and well. The last time we spoke, my father still owned The Siren's Call, I believe."

Finn waggled his thick red brows. "Aye, was a fine establishment. I enjoyed meself many nights 'ere."

She pursed her lips in an unconvincing attempt to smile. "Huh, yes. I'm sure you did. As did many pigs of men my father let through the doors."

She tossed the dagger down on the desk where it hit with a loud *ting*. Roselyn then plopped down into the massive brown leather wingback behind the desk with a tired sigh. "So, you have no spoils to claim? No treasure to protect?"

Henry cleared his throat. "No, we do not."

"Well, then. I can't very well make you pay a duty, now. Can I?" The woman's words sounded reassuring, but I still felt uneased. Roselyn then added, "Regardless. You tried to avoid coming to see me, Henry, and that disappoints me. I don't think I can let that slide. What if others take stake? No, I have to make an example out of you all."

"What do you propose?" Henry asked, the raspy tone of his low and impatient voice carrying through the room.

"Three favors," Roselyn replied.

"Three?" Finn spat. "Bloody Christ!"

"One," Henry countered. His arms crossed tightly.

The woman narrowed her eyes as she seemed to contemplate it. "Two."

"Fine. Two favors." Henry stepped forward and reached out a hand. They shook on it.

My stomach turned at the thought of us owing this woman anything. What were the extents of the favors? Could Roselyn Wallace quite literally ask for anything? But, as Henry turned to come back to where I was, I was given my answer before he even sat down.

"Excellent." Wallace clapped her hands once. "I have a task for you to do. The first favor, if you will."

He stopped, eyes locked on mine in a plead of forgiveness, and spun back around to face her.

"I'm throwing a big party this evening," she began. "A Christmas party. My four barrels of wine are stuck on a merchant vessel just a few yards off the coast. The ship is having some trouble with its sails. I need a group of men to row out, help fix them, so the ship can come to shore and deliver my wine. Can you do that for me?"

"Yes," Henry replied and glanced back to where I sat. "But, does the merchant vessel not have row boats of its own?"

"No, they foolishly left them behind to make room for more cargo," Wallace replied.

Henry exchanged a knowing glance with Gus. "Just allow me the time to take Dianna back to our room at the tavern."

I sprang upright. "What? No. I'm coming with you."

"Absolutely not," he told me. "You passed out. Clearly you need to rest."

"I'm fine now," I pleaded. "I swear."

Lottie took a seat next to me. "Dianna, I have to side with Henry on this. Yours and the baby's safety is the most important thing. You can't be rowing out to sea in a little boat."

Part of me wanted to pull rank, play the captain card and demand I come along. But I knew that would only alert Roselyn Wallace that I was the real captain of The Queen and Henry had been pretty insistent she be kept in the dark. So, like a child, I crossed my arms and leaned back against the chaise with a harrumph.

"Dianna is more than welcome to stay here and wait for your return," Wallace suggested. The woman spoke about me as if I were a child, or not in the room at all. And then I realized what the source of my unease was about her. She wouldn't make eye contact with me.

I couldn't tell if she was truly being sincere in the offer. Perhaps it was the tinge of jealousy running through my veins, but I could have sworn I caught the glimmer of something in her eye. Deception? No...something else. I couldn't put my finger on it. But Lottie must have sensed it, too.

"Thank you for the kind gesture, but that's quite alright," my best friend replied for me. "I'll take Dianna back to the tavern. I could use some rest myself." She turned back, her blonde hair shielding her face like a curtain as she threw me a playful wink.

"I'll return as soon as I can," Henry promised as he helped me to my feet.

It killed me to let him go. All I wanted since finding his mother's ring was to haul Henry off somewhere private and share in the joy I knew he'd feel. But I also knew that Wallace was letting us off easy and I had to play along.

I held his gaze and willed him to feel my anxious heart. "*Right* back. Promise?"

The line of his mouth widened. "Promise."

From the other side of the room, I heard Wallace clear her throat. "Of course, you're all invited to attend the party tonight." She had a playful smirk on her face as she rushed the words from her mouth. "As my guests."

Henry sighed. "That's really not necess –"

"I insist." Her response was curt and rushed but the woman eased before adding, "All the food and drink you could dream of."

"Aye, finally," Finn churred, "now yer talkin'." His cheerful expression relaxed as he caught my discreet glare and he shrugged apologetically.

"I'm sure after your long journey, you could all use a good time," Wallace continued not taking no for an answer.

Damn, she was persistent.

Part of me wondered what she'd do if we really pushed back and declined her invitation. Would it piss her off? Was she one of those unstable beautiful people? Did the power of her position weigh heavy in her pretty head? I didn't know enough about Wallace and, from what I could guess, Henry kept details from me for a reason. Another part of me, the seedy jealous bit, wanted nothing more than to dig deeper and figure out the past Henry shared with the dark goddess.

"We'll be there," I blurted out. My crew turned and shot me a look of disbelief. Except Finn, who rocked back on his heels in pure joy. The promise of a feast and endless alcohol was enough to lure him into a bear's cave, I would imagine. But, then I realized, I wasn't supposed to make calls like that. I wasn't the captain. "Uh, if it's alright with Captain Barrett, of course."

Henry's chest heaved at the face of defeat. What else could he do with Finn and I rooting to go? "A party it is, then."

"Excellent!" Wallace declared and hopped up from her chair. "Guests will arrive at eight." She fetched a quill from her desk and scribbled down ink on a loose piece of parchment before handing it to Henry. "This is the number on my cargo. I'll have Angus bring the carriages around and he'll you escorted back to the docks. He'll also show you to the rowboat."

We followed as she exited the room, Henry close behind her with me in tow, our hands linked tightly. When our group reached the foyer, Roselyn turned and laid her hand on Henry's shoulder. Her slender brown fingers and perfectly manicured nails caressing the curve of his arm a little too much for my liking. An unexpected flare of jealousy burned through my chest.

"I'll have my seamstress send something to The Kraken's Den for you to wear," she told him with a seductive tone that soured my stomach. Her eyes raking over his body. *My* man's body. "You still look about the same size."

Henry, realizing her discreet advance, gently pulled away. "Thank you, I appreciate it, but it's truly not –"

"Again, I insist." She crossed her arms, causing the exposed cleavage to heave. "When have you ever known me to take no for an answer?" Roselyn then glanced in my direction, as if suddenly realizing I was standing there, and grinned maliciously. "I can have

The Siren's Call

something sent for you as well, Dianna. Something to fit over that lovely belly of yours."

I wanted to yank the silky black waves from her damn head and step on her perfect face. But I squashed the jealous rage and pulled Henry close to me, resting my head against his shoulder.

"That won't be necessary, Roselyn." I held my smile as her eyes narrowed at the use of her first name, something I sensed she didn't like. "I'll take care of mine and Henry's outfits for the party while he's fetching your wine."

All of my suspicions about Wallace's intentions or the past she shared with Henry were confirmed in one single glare. Her deep brown eyes bore into mine, mirroring my jealousy but quickly faded away with hopelessness. I may have been jealous of her beauty, but Henry was *mine*, a comforting fact I carried with me all the way to the carriage.

Henry gripped my hand as I placed a foot on the first step, but gave it a gentle tug before I could get in. "Don't you think you should rest when you return?"

"No, I'm fine," I told him. And I really was. The sense of something to prove kickstarted my energy once again. I grinned and tugged at the collar of his leather trench, bringing his face to mine. "Don't worry, I'll get you something nice to wear."

He failed to hide his look of concern. "Dianna," Henry's voice lowered just above a whisper, "You have nothing to prove."

My eyebrow arched, and I leaned in to place a long, sensual kiss that I knew would linger on his lips until we met again later that night. My hand slipped inside his jacket and squeezed the hard muscles of his back, pressing my chest against him. I pulled away and delighted in the fire that had lit in Henry's hungry gaze, then threw a challenging glance over his shoulder to Wallace who stood seething in jealousy on her front porch. He may have been mine, but I didn't trust that woman. And my instincts had never steered me wrong before.

I took the second step and held Henry's gaze as I let go of his hand and smirked. "Don't I?"

CHAPTER FIVE

I scrambled out of the carriage, leaving behind the awkward silence that had filled it on the way back to The Kraken's Den. Lottie tried to strike up general chit chat, I could tell she felt bad for the way things went down at Wallace's. But I was pissed. Not at her. Well, not entirely, anyway. I just felt betrayed. Blindsided. How could my crew not tell me about the gorgeous, dark goddess that clearly has a thing for the man I'm in love with? How could Lottie have not told me? Given me a heads up, at the very least. I stormed through the tavern, bypassing the curious innkeeper for the stairs.

"Dianna," Lottie called at my back. I didn't reply. "Dianna!"

I stopped on the first stair and spun around. "What?"

"Why are you angry with me?"

"I'm not angry," I told my friend. Her face twisted in confusion. "I'm just...I feel like a fool."

Tears unexpectedly began to pool in my eyes and Lottie quickly jumped to the stair on which I stood and wrapped a comforting arm around me.

"Oh, Dianna, I'm so sorry. Come on, let's go upstairs."

We entered the room I shared with Henry and I paced the floor, trying to keep in the emotions that had rushed to the surface. Where did they come from? I was fine. Full of energy and a burning desire to show up Roselyn Wallace at her own party. Now I was threatening myself to fall apart.

Stupid pregnancy hormones.

Lottie opened her mouth to speak but I beat her to it. "How could you not tell me?"

She shook her head. "Tell you what?"

"About *her*!" I cawed. "That Wallace was actually *Roselyn* Wallace. Beautiful, flawless, and clearly in love with Henry! I was completely blindsided. I wasn't prepared for that entire experience."

My flailing hands flew in the air around me as I paced some more. Lottie sighed and rubbed her face tiredly before taking a step in my direction. Gently, her sturdy hands took my shaking ones and held them tightly.

"Dianna," my friend said softly but sternly. "I've never met the woman before in my life. Didn't even know she was a woman at all. My father had never let me go with him and, from what I can tell, when he paid a trip to see Wallace and square up his dues, it was her father. It's been years since I've been back here, she would have been a young girl then, too."

"But she knew who you were," I replied, a little calmer.

"What do you mean?"

"Outside, when we first arrived," I began, "She glanced around and said she recognized everyone's faces except mine."

Lottie couldn't have faked the pure look of bewilderment that spread across her face. "I-I have no idea, Dianna. I swear. Please believe that."

I closed my eyes and inhaled deeply. "I do."

I immediately felt bad for tearing into my best friend the way I did, the relief that flushed from her body was hard not to notice.

"It appears that, perhaps, the men in our lives have some explaining to do, though," she added.

I pinched the bridge of my nose. "Yeah."

"I can pry Augustus for information," Lottie offered. "See what sort of past Wallace and Henry may have had."

"No, no," I told her. I'd ask him myself.

I chewed at my bottom lip as I pondered. What if I never got the full truth from him? He'd kept a lot of details about the woman from me already. Clearly there was something he felt was worth hiding.

"Actually, yes." I regretted the words as soon as I spoke them.

Lottie raised her eyebrows in surprise. "Really?"

I let out a slight moan of annoyed agony. "No, don't. I'll ask Henry myself. I should give him the chance to explain. I should trust him to tell me the truth."

"I wish I had that sort of faith in men," she said jokingly and took a seat at the small dinette table in the middle of the room. She plucked a grape from the bowl of fruit and popped it in her mouth. "She's hideous, you know. Absolutely wretched to look at."

I rolled my eyes at my friend's attempt to cheer me up. "No, she's not. Far from it. She's like some kind of goddess. I've never seen a more beautiful woman." I glanced down at my enormous stomach and felt my feet swelling in the tight leather boots I wore. "How can I compete with that?"

Lottie whipped a grape and it flicked off my forehead.

"Ow! What was that for?"

"Will you just listen to yourself?" she said and stood to come meet me. "She may be a beautiful goddess, but you're a glorious queen. You and *you* alone carry Henry's heart as well as his child inside your body. You traveled three hundred years to save him from death. You stuck by him when his mind turned to darkness and helped him see the light. His entire world lies with *you*, Dianna."

Her words brought tears to my eyes as she placed reassuring hands on my shoulders and grinned triumphantly.

"What you should be asking yourself is how can *she* compete with that."

***

After we got cleaned up, Lottie and I descended the stairs to the bustling tavern below. The scent of delicious food floated through the air as hungry guests waited about. Some sat at the bar near the rear of the building, others stood and sat around the common areas. Basking in the warmth of the fireplace, relaxing in the cozy chairs. I spotted Charlie, Seamus, and John gathered around a large round table, mugs of ale on their hands.

I gave Charlie a mock motherly eyebrow as I approached. "Don't drink too much, now, boys."

Charlie put down the wooden mug and wiped his mouth. Seamus replied. "No, Ma'am, uh, Captain. Just wetting our lips while we wait for supper."

"I'm just kidding," I replied and tousled the dirty blonde hair atop Charlie's head as I took a seat next to him and across from the other two.

Lottie leaned against the table. "What have you boys been up to? Haven't seen much of you around."

John, the older one, replied dutifully. "Been keepin' an eye on The Queen, Ma'am. And finishin' up the last few repairs Gus gave us to do."

"Excellent," she told them proudly and shifted to face the table better. "We'll need you to stick close to the tavern tonight. Dianna and I will be attending a party with Gus, Finn, and Henry. We'll need eyes on our belongings while we're away."

The three nodded, eager to please. Charlie's slender hand gently touched my arm, catching my attention.

"Yes?" I said.

He twisted in his chair and pulled a small notebook from his trouser pocket and laid it on the table.

"Aw, come on, mate," said Seamus. "You don't need that anymore. We understand ya just fine."

Charlie's cheeks flushed red as he regarded me from the side. Why did he seem so self-conscious all of a sudden? I didn't comment, for fear of embarrassing him further. I only waited patiently with an encouraging smile. Charlie tightened the collar of his loose shirt around his neck and cleared his throat.

"M-my mother," he spoke with a still strained voice, cheeks reddening further.

It took a moment, but I remembered what he asked me while The Queen was still at sea. "Oh, of course, Charlie. I promised to take you to your mother, and I will. I swear. Things have just been a little...chaotic since we came here." I leaned in and whispered, trying to make him feel privileged to information, even though our small party could hear. "We've got a trail on Maria."

I thought he'd smile or seem relieved, but the young man's face paled and I watched as his hand mindlessly gripped the collar of his shirt even tighter. He flipped open the notebook and licked a worn-down lead before writing one word.

Soon?

My heart gave one hard beat as I realized the anxiety he clearly harbored about Maria. Hiding the massive scar across his neck, refusing to use his voice. He must have deeply missed his mother and ached to go see her, especially now that we were so close.

"You know, I won't make you stay if you wish to go, Charlie." I pat the back of his hand gingerly. "If you'd like to go home, you can."

He didn't answer, only hung his head after pocketing the notebook and lead.

"With all due respect, Captain" John spoke from across the table. "I believe Charlie here really wanted to bring you with him. I think," he paused and eyed Charlie, as if asking permission to continue, "he wants his mum to meet the woman who saved his life."

My eyes welled with tears and I looked to my young friend. His sorrowful expression confirmed John's words. I was suddenly regretting how much I'd ignored him since docking in Southampton and was grateful for the friendship he'd obviously formed with John and Seamus. Apparently, he even felt comfortable enough to speak around them. But why would he still feel self-conscious about speaking in front of me?

"Charlie," I said just barely above a whisper, for that was all I could manage without crying in front of everyone in The Kraken's Den. "You are the one who saved *me*. That night in the woods. I owe you my life. Helping to heal your wound was the least I could do repay the sacrifice you made for me."

Shakily, he smiled proudly.

"Nevertheless," I continued. "I'd be honored to meet your mother and tell her how amazing her boy is." I leaned back in the chair and glanced at Lottie who gave me a shrug. I heaved a sigh. "Just give me a few days, okay?"

Charlie nodded, but had a hopeful look on his face.

"If I make it through this party tonight and learn more about Maria's whereabouts, then I promise to take you home."

Just then, the innkeeper came to our table with three massive plates of food. "Hello, boys," he greeted happily. "Sorry for the long wait, I'm afraid it's just me and the cook here tonight."

Seamus immediately began to dig into the pile of cooked vegetables and meat covered in gravy. John looked up at the innkeeper respectfully. "No wait a'tall, Mister Cresley."

Cresley. I hadn't even asked the innkeeper his name. How horribly negligent of me. I'd been so preoccupied with finding Maria that I forgotten everything else.

"Ladies, can I get you anything?" the kind man asked Lottie and I.

I stood and then pushed in my chair. "No, thank you," I told him as Lottie came to my side. "I was just checking in with my boys. I truly appreciate you tending to them in my absence, Mister Cresley. If there's anything you need help with around the tavern, they'd be happy to help you, I'm sure." I cast the three young men a motion over my shoulder and their food stuffed faces nodded in agreement.

"Especially tonight. You said you were short-handed. Charlotte and I have to head out in search of some dresses, so —"

"Dresses, you say?" Cresley inquired. "What sort?"

"Fancy ones, for a big party over at The Siren's Call," Lottie told him with a huff and rolled her blue eyes.

"Ah, yes, that one," the tall, slender man said knowingly and rubbed his chin. "Wallace is well known for her annual Yule Dinner and Dance." He gave a friendly chuckle. "Seems to get bigger and fancier each year. I imagine you lovely ladies will be wantin' beautiful gowns. Any ol' dress just won't do. Especially with your lovely belly to consider."

I rubbed a hand over my large stomach. "Yes, but we can't exactly be picky on such short notice. The party is in a few hours."

Mister Cresley shook his head. "Nonsense. I'll have my driver take you to a wonderful tailor with the most magnificent formal wear. She'll fit you on the spot." The old man's eyes glistened as he grinned widely. "She'll make you look like queens."

Lottie and I exchanged a look of surprise before I turned back to our new friend with a grin.

"Sounds perfect."

***

Mister Cresley's personal driver, an extremely tall and broad man, much the same build as Henry, happily drove the carriage through Southampton toward Market Square. He went around another way than Lottie and I had earlier, leading the horse-drawn buggy to the upper area where the apothecary was and the fancier stores. I glanced out the quaint little window as we circled the large stone fountain which sat in the center and came to a stop. The carriage jostled as the driver jumped down from his seat and graciously opened the door for us. I gripped his outstretched hand tightly as I stepped down to the cobblestone below.

"Thank you," I told him and smiled.

He turned and helped Lottie out. "You're most welcome, Miss. The store Mister Cresley spoke about is just right there."

I followed his motioned gaze toward the storefront I spotted before, with the stunning silk dresses and glistening jewelry boasting in the large window.

"Madam Guthrie is the best there is. They says she can work magic with those ol' fingers of hers. You're in good hands, I reckon. And you needn't worry. Take your time, I shall await your return right here." He tipped his flat cap and jumped back up in his seat with ease.

Lottie raised her thin blonde brows. "Well, she'd best have magic fingers to find a fancy dress to my liking." She looped her arm through mine and led us toward the shop. "Bloody fabric prisons, they are. Too big. Always have to be watchin' where you step so the dress doesn't knock things over. Ridiculous."

My friend heaved on the heavy wooden door, the tiny bell hung overhead jingling as she did. We stepped inside, taken aback by the endless rows of hung garments and vertical displays of handbags and other accessories. Mesmerizing jewel tones painted a dark rainbow throughout the space, reflecting the ample lantern light with silks and other radiant textiles.

"How can I help you two beauties?" a croaky old smoker's voice sounded from the back of the shop.

We stood and watched as the wave of movement made its way through the stacks of bags and layers of hung garments until the body of a tiny old woman emerged in front of us. She couldn't have been more than four feet tall. Cream colored silks hung loosely from her teeny frame, her neck adorned with rows and rows of pearls. A pair of dainty, wired framed specs sat in the bridge of her long nose. The woman was like something out of a children's fairy tale. The quirky and wise old lady.

"Madam Guthrie, I presume?" I offered my hand and she took it, the abnormally long and crooked fingers of hers wrapping around mine.

"Yes," she croaked happily and squinted up at our faces. "Let me guess, you're in need of dresses for tonight's Yule Dinner and Dance."

Lottie's face paled as her widened eyes looked to me. Unable to hide my own surprise at the woman's perception, I let out a laugh. "You're as wise as you appear, Madam. You would be correct. But, as you can imagine, we need something quick."

Lottie caught sight of something to our right and she pointed to a small section of menswear. "And perhaps a couple of men's suits, as well."

"Certainly," she replied. "Do you know their measurements?"

"I can take a guess," Lottie told her and shrugged. "For Augustus, anyway."

The two women awaited my response and I chewed at my bottom lip in thought. Henry would definitely need something to wear. And he'd be out taking care of Wallace's favor until the party. But I didn't have the faintest idea what his measurements were. I glanced out the window at our carriage and grinned.

"Would you mind fetching the driver?" I asked Lottie.

She didn't seem to understand but asked no questions, regardless. She ran outside, blonde hair swaying back and forth as she did, and I watched as my friend chatted with the driver for a quick moment and then returned with him. His large frame entered the shop and he politely removed his hat, holding it to his chest.

"Is everything alright, Miss White?"

I still wasn't used to that, hearing Henry's true name spoken with such ease. I didn't bother to correct him, to say that I'd yet to inherit the name. I smiled. "I never did get your name."

"Cillian, Miss."

"Cillian, you're just about the same height and build as my fiancé, Henry." I paused to laugh. "Would you mind trying on some garments for me?"

He appeared hesitant, but dutifully accepted with a nod. "Of course, Miss."

I made a mental note to give Cillian a nice tip when we arrived back at the Den. Madam Guthrie showed us an array of options for men's suits, pulling them out from piles and racks of bottomless clothing. She seemed to know every single article of cloth in the shop and we watched with amusement as her tiny body sometimes disappeared among the hanging dresses and jackets. Finally, after poor Cillian had tried on a dozen outfits, I had found the perfect suit for Henry. Black cotton trousers, black leather vest and matching pea coat that fit snuggly over a stark white blouse and neck scarf. I could just imagine how handsome he'd look in it.

Lottie plucked a tan suede coat with a dark brown vest that appeared to be some sort of silk for Gus. I tried to stifle the giggle that forced its way out at the thought of her getting him to wear something so fancy. Then my mind went to a side note. Finn.

"Madam Guthrie, would you happen to have something appropriate for a Scotsman to wear?" I motioned with my head toward the door where Cillian had just slipped out. "For someone a little larger than Cillian?"

Her beady eyes widened behind the teeny specs. "Larger? Good grief, are you dressing a Scotsman or a giant?"

Lottie and I exchanged a knowing glance and I laughed. "A bit of both. He's a big man. I'd understand if you don't have anything on such short notice."

"Nonsense. I've yet to turn someone away undressed." The old woman waggled her bony fingers. "Madam Guthrie has something for everyone, dearie."

She weaved her way to the back of the store, leaving Lottie and I standing in wait. We wandered around, picking at random dresses, all beautiful in their own way but none that appealed to me. Too poufy, too small, too much color, not enough color. I was beginning to lose hope of ever finding something nice enough to wow the socks off Henry but also narrow the jealous eyes of Roselyn Wallace. Finally, after about fifteen minutes, Madam Guthrie returned with a few thick garments draped over her short arm. Plaid in color.

"Do you know the Scot's clan?" she asked us.

"His clan?" I questioned back.

Lottie cleared her throat. "Finn's last name. It depicts which Scottish clan he comes from. He doesn't share much of himself outside his life aboard the ship, though. And I've never seen his tartan before."

Clan. Tartan. These were new terms to me and I suddenly felt like a horrible friend. But then I recalled my first encounter with Wallace. Yeah, my ears may have filled with the pounding of my anxious heart, but I still remember hearing her address Finn by his full name.

"Finnigan Artair, is his name," I told them both.

"Aha, excellent!" Madam Guthrie exclaimed and began sifting through the hefty layers on her arm. "I have the Clan Artair hunting tartan but also this more traditional, common cloth." She pulled out a gorgeous, vibrant green plaid with bright yellow and gold stripes. "This one's already made into a kilt and should fit a man of large proportions."

I shook my head in astonishment. "It's perfect. I'll take it."

"Wonderful," she replied and opened a large, wooden chest near our feet. "You'll also need these."

She pulled out long white socks, a neatly folded green jacket with gold buttons, and a crisp off-white shirt. I graciously accepted the items and laid them on top of the kilt before setting them aside with Henry's outfit.

"Now, dearies," she said and clasped her hands together. "It's time to dress the both of your gorgeous bodies. Have your eyes caught anything of interest?"

"I'd prefer something that isn't too...large," Lottie told her and motioned at her sides with her hands. "I'd very much like to move without needing a wide girth of space around me." She chewed at her lip in thought. "And nothing too colorful."

Madam Guthrie nodded slowly, rubbing at her chin as she looked Lottie up and down. She hummed and hawed as her tiny hands with long fingers picked at Lottie's body, lifting her arms and cinching her waist.

"What a fine specimen you are," the woman croaked as she flipped up the bottom of Lottie's plain brown skirt and measured the long legs underneath. "Are you sure you don't want something in an emerald?" She stood and pushed up the spectacles on her nose. "Or a lovely sapphire blue?"

Lottie's face twisted in annoyance. "No, nothing too color –"

"Sapphire blue." The woman's bob of grey hair disappeared to the left side of the shop like a little rabbit sprinting into the forest.

"No, Madam Guthrie!" Lottie called after her.

"Just trust me, child!"

Her raspy voice seemed to come from all around the store as it echoed off the many surfaces and I laughed. Lottie turned to me, unamused.

"This little witch lady is going to make me look ridiculous."

"Have a little faith," I told my friend. "I mean, look how she just *had* the perfect things for Henry, Gus, and Finn. I'm sure she knows how to dress you."

Lottie rolled her eyes and crossed her arms tightly. "Yes, a little too perfect, don't you think?"

I stole a glance in the general direction that Madam Guthrie had disappeared and stepped closer to Lottie, voice lowered to a whisper. "What do you mean?"

"I've been all over the world with my father," she spoke quiet and quick. "And never have I ever come across a tailor or shop that just happens to have exactly what you want. Or the measurements you need. It's just unheard of."

I let her words stew in my brain. It *was* a little too perfect.

"You think she's really a witch?"

"What of it?" Madam Guthrie spoke as she appeared seemingly out of nowhere, a heap of dark blue silk draped over her shoulder.

Startled, both Lottie and I scrambled for words. The woman let out a loud, raspy cackle.

"No, dearies, a witch I am not. More of a collector. A curator of the unusual. Sure, one can step into any tailor and have a garment made just for them." She paused and fanned her hand around the space where we stood surrounded by mountains of items. "But in my store, the perfect outfit is already waiting."

"Apologies, Madam, I meant no disrespect." Lottie blushed as she hung her head.

"No need for that," the woman assured and then yanked the dress from her shoulder. "We have you two pretty little things to dress and very little time to do so. I may be a miracle worker and tailor quickly, but I *am* still human." She threw Lottie a playful smirk. "Regardless of what some may say."

Lottie pursed her lips and eyeballed the dress. "I really appreciate you helping us on such short notice, Madam Guthrie, and I'm sure the dress is beautiful, but I just don't −"

"You, dearie, will wear this stunning creation of sapphire and love it. I Promise." Before Lottie could respond, Madam Guthrie added, "Just omit the pannier and you won't have to worry about the space you occupy."

Lottie held the words in her mouth for a moment, wanting so desperately to argue against the dress she clearly thought was far too fancy. But she let it go.

"Now, my pregnant brunette. What shall you wear?"

I swallowed hard against the dryness of my throat as the woman circled my body, sizing everything up and taking stock of what she had to work with. I'd already had a look around and saw nothing even remotely close to something that would fit me properly without looking like an undesirable maid.

"You've got quite the neck," she observed. "Long and dainty. But a frame that's strong. And that hair." She clucked her tongue. "Like dark chocolate."

"I have to look..." I suddenly felt self-conscious at the thought of admitting my goal. "I don't want to necessarily hide the fact that I'm with child. I know that's almost impossible at this point, and it's not something I care to hide, anyway. I just want to look...I hope to find a dress that will –"

"Be the envy of every woman in the room?" Madam Guthrie finished for me with a cocked eyebrow.

I felt my cheeks flush. "No...just one."

She beckoned Lottie with a curl of one long, bony finger over to a stack of large flattop trunks. I watched as they removed the top two, leaving just one short and wide box with gaudy brass hardware. Lottie came back and stood next to me as Madam Guthrie fished a key from a full ring at her side and unlocked the trunk. The top creaked as it opened, and the woman reached into to pull out a beautiful silk dress. Red as fresh blood and a black corset to top it off. I hadn't a clue what I wanted until I laid eyes on the dress she held up in her hands.

Now it was as if it were the very thing I'd been searching for.

"This was worn by the Duchess of Devonshire on her birthday and during her first pregnancy. A few simple alterations to the waistline and the boning is all it requires. It was made for you, dearie."

I was at a loss for words. "Madam Guthrie..."

"Say no more." She waved at the air between the three of us. "Go, head back to your rooms and soak in a bath. Pin those gorgeous locks. I'll make the alterations as quickly as I can and have everything sent over to The Kraken's Den before you leave for the party."

"We can't thank you enough," I told her. "Do let us know how much the cost is and I'll have payment squared up." With a mighty tip, I added to myself. "Are you sure you can have the alterations done within the next couple of hours?"

She opened the front door and ushered us out. "A couple of hours? I could have it done twice over."

We listened to her raspy cackle as the door closed behind us and Lottie leaned into me to whisper, "Told you. Witch."

I playfully pushed at her arm and laughed as we strolled toward a patiently awaiting Cillian. Witch or not, the old gypsy-like seamstress was the answer to my prayers. I gloated inwardly at the thought of Henry's face when he would see me in that dress. And, better yet, Roselyn Wallace's face when she realized I wasn't to be messed with. Like Lottie said, she was no competition. Captain Devil Eyed Barrett only had eyes for me. He was mine, and mine alone.

And tonight, I would make sure of it.

CHAPTER SIX

My head lulled back as I relaxed in the hot bath that sat in my room. Steam billowed up from the surface and mixed with the cool air, soaking into my skin. The events of the day played out in my mind and I went through them over and over like a short movie on repeat.

I'd awoke that same morning feeling lost. That I might never find Maria and save my mother. England was a huge country, and she could have been anywhere. Heck, she could have fled to Ireland and Scotland by now. But, no, she was close by. I just knew it. No matter how much the thought seethed in my veins, I was connected to the psychopath by blood and something deep inside my core told me she was here. That, strangely enough, she was...*waiting* for me.

I wasn't scared. Not anymore. I carried with me a heavy fear of finding my sister, and my mother, for months. The only thing keeping me going was sheer determination and a will to do what was right. Well, that and Henry. My constant. My everything. I rubbed a gentle hand over my growing belly and silently cooed to the baby inside.

Our baby.

I left behind dark thoughts of my sibling and dreamed of the life Henry and I would have together when this was all over. A life on land, just as he promised. I had no idea he felt that way, that he missed his old life so much. But Henry William White was a simple boy with a love for both the land and sea. The life of piracy was something forced upon him and he had no choice but to conform and adapt. To embrace the lifestyle. I see that now. He'd become Devil Eyed Barrett out of necessity. It was his way of surviving. My gorgeous pirate king. God, the very thought of his brooding stare, those black eyes boring into my soul. My heart. The blonde scruff of his sharp jaw smoothing against my face and the deep, raspy growl I so often fished for as my fingers traced the lines of Henry's muscular chest.

I quietly writhed in the tub, eyes closed, and head thrown back as my hands explored my new, ever-changing body. It still called for him, like a siren's song. My tender breasts heaved as I let out a moan and lifted a foot to the edge of the tub.

"Now, isn't that a glorious sight?" spoke a voice from the doorway.

I let out a yelp and sunk down into the tub, covering my body. I willed my face to stop flushing crimson as my eyes found him, though. "Jesus, Henry. Some warning would be nice."

His mouth widened to the side with a half grin as he turned and closed the door behind him. "And miss the sight of you pleasuring yourself? Never."

His tall frame sauntered toward the tub, black eyes locked on mine. They burned with a deep desire that I hadn't realized I craved to see until that very moment. His need for me. I watched hungrily as Henry removed his clothing, piece by piece. The leather trench crumpled to the floor, followed by the heavy clank of a sword and big, leather boots. My heart thumped faster, harder as he seductively slipped off the soiled white shirt and revealed the lithe muscles underneath. My hands twitched and ached to touch him. Henry then stepped into the tub by my feet and lowered himself down into the warm water.

"You're back early," I pointed out.

"Is that a bad thing?" He took one of my feet and lifted it to his lips, placing kisses along the inside of my ankle.

"No, just an observation," I replied and felt my nipples harden as his lips climbed the length of my leg. "I got you something to wear."

"Did you, now?" Henry answered mindlessly, preoccupied with the pink skin of my inner thigh.

"Yes, black, your favorite color," I said cheekily.

"You know me well." His fingers traced the creases around my hips and upper thigh.

"D-did everything go alright with the wine barrels?"

I felt his mouth grin against my skin at my falter.

"Yes, the tide was on our side and we rowed quickly." My leg returned to the comfort of the warm water as Henry shifted and moved closer, positioning himself between my thighs, face only inches from mine. "But, I reckon if I knew I had this waiting for me I would have jumped overboard and swam back."

I grabbed hold of his face and closed the few inches between us, touching my forehead to his. "If I had my way, I never would have let you go in the first place."

"Everything was fine," he assured me. "You've got nothin' to worry about."

I grabbed hold of his jaw and forced his gaze upward. "You swear? I have nothing to be concerned about? Nothing from your past that I should know?"

"Nothing from my past matters anymore. Not now. Not ever. So long as I'm with you." His eyes urged me to believe. "I swear it."

In response I rolled my hips upward. "Good."

Henry moaned in delight, and my body felt the vibration of that deep, throaty growl. "It'll be over soon. All of it. And then we can spend the rest of our lives in bed together."

Even though the very thought was silly, I joined Henry in the fantasy. Anchored in the moment, it was just him and I. My writhing body, his able hands, and the subtle splash of hot water in the silence of our candlelit room.

***

It was well past eight o'clock and I worried that Wallace would be displeased with us showing up late. But I quickly reminded myself that she'd have to understand, given the short notice she'd allotted us to get ready for such an event. Considering we'd only had a few hours to find proper formalwear, I think we done alright.

I twisted and turned in the long mirror of my room, admiring the way the stunning dress flowed to the floor in a thick curtain of red silk, and the way the altered black corset curved above my pregnant belly and hugged what little torso I had left. Madam Guthrie took some liberty with the neckline and altered it to a plunging dip which showed off my heaving bosom. That woman really could work magic with those boney fingers of hers.

From my velvet satchel, I fetched Henry's mother's ring. All day I'd been dying to show him, to see that joy on his face. I knew we'd be wed soon, but I also knew how desperately he wished for his mother's wedding ring on my finger.

Suddenly, the door opened, and Henry peeked in. "Are you ready to –"

His hand slipped from the handle and I relished in the way his eyes widened at the very sight of me.

"Christ," he said in a whisper of awe and entered the room fully. He looked painfully good in the outfit I chose for him. "You're stunning, Dianna. That dress. You're a vision of a goddess." Henry stopped in front of me and gleamed down at my warming cheeks. "I'd be a smart man to not let you out of my sight tonight."

The ring pressed against the skin of my clenched and nervous palm. "Tonight? Or forever?" I asked him, preparing myself to reveal the treasure I'd found.

"Forever is a given, my pirate queen."

He tipped my chin and placed a soft, sensual kiss on my quivering lips. God, the man sure knew how to fill my head with clouds. I fought through the fog as he pulled away and opened my mouth to speak but was interrupted by the abrupt opening of the door.

"Aye, blood Christ!" Finn spewed loudly. "Is we goin' yet, or what? My belly craves the heavy weight of wine and good grub."

"Finn," I said, forgetting the initial annoyance I felt at his intrusion as I took in the dapper sight of him. Decked out with the Artair tartan and outfit I'd gotten for him, Finn looked like a proper Scottish gentleman. If a thing ever existed. "You look so handsome!"

He gave a mock expression of gloating as he tugged at the collar of his emerald jacket and smoothed the freshly cleaned hair of his long, red beard. "That's *Sir* Finn Artair, to ye poppers."

He dropped the act and we all shared a lighthearted laugh. But my friend's face quickly turned serious and those big green eyes glistened with appreciation. "Thank ye, Captain. 'Tis been many years since I laid eyes on me clan's colors. It fills me heart with pride to wear it."

"Well, it looks great on you," I told him.

"Is everyone ready to go?" Henry asked.

"Aye, ready and waitin'," Finn replied dutifully and waggled his big, red eyebrows. "Let's clean this wench out of French wine and delight in the feast, for tomorrow is another day and we've got ourselves a devil to catch."

I inhaled deeply and exchanged a glance with Henry before we followed Finn to the stairs. Yes, tonight may be filled with yuletide celebration, but I would truly celebrate once I put a stop to my sister. Tonight was a matter of obligation, to keep the peace with Wallace as we searched for Maria. A fact that never truly left my mind. Or Henry's, I realized from the way the look in his eyes seemed to mirror mine.

I had to have faith that my wish was conspiring with the universe to work its magic. That I'd eventually be brought to Maria and save my mother from the dark fate that chased her. I wondered, as I descended the stairs to the tavern below, if Mom knew her what her daughters were doing. That one hunted her down while the other fought to save her. Was she tucked safely away with the Celtic witches? Or did she reside somewhere out in the open, vulnerable to her possible fate?

I brushed those thoughts from my mind, knowing I had no control over them or their answers. All I had was the present, the truth in my hands and the tangible reality to which I lived in each day. Henry, my crew, my friends. Family. And the child growing inside of me. Discreetly, I tucked the ring into my bosom for later, where it would wait for the perfect moment to tell Henry. We all piled into horse-drawn carriages and trolleyed along toward The Siren's Call. This time, Henry and I sharing a space with Finn while Lottie and Gus took the second.

The crisp December night smelled of frost and fireplaces. Each lamppost burned with the flame of a lantern and cast just the right amount of light on the Christmas wreaths that hung from each one. A delicate sprinkle of snow fell from the sky and melted as it hit the dirt road beneath us. I wrapped the fur collar of my cloak tight around my neck and leaned into Henry's shoulder.

Across from us, Finn gleamed. "Aye, 'tis good to see ye so happy."

"It feels wrong to be going to a party when I have such a heavy responsibility hanging over my head. I'll be much happier when this is over, and we won't have Maria Cobham to worry about ever again," I told him.

"Are ye sure ye made the wish and didn't just dream it?" Finn replied. He spoke with a layer of humor, but I knew underneath he had concerns.

"No, it's working," I assured them both. "I can...*feel* it. Like a strange tugging inside my chest."

"What about your first wish, then?" Henry asked.

"What do you mean?"

"You say you can feel something pulling you in the right direction to Maria or, at least, a sense of it working." He let a pause hang in the air between us. "But, you first wished for your friend Benjamin to be set free. Is there anything telling you that it was successful? Or that the wish is carrying out as it should?"

I chewed at my bottom lip, as I always did when deep in thought. I knew Henry had reservations about Benjamin and how the pirate showed obvious affection toward me. But I had assured him time and time again that Benjamin was only a friend. A dear friend who I'd gone through a great ordeal with and shared an otherworldly bond with. But a friend, nonetheless. He couldn't hold a candle to Henry.

But this was about something else. The strike of worry on both the men's faces told me that it was more about my second wish, and whether or not it really was coming true. I thought about Benjamin and The Black Soul. Sure, I worried my wish didn't work, but that was only due to the fact I had no evidence to prove otherwise. But when I imagined my friend, his massive frame topped with a smirk that softened his grim face, I felt somewhere deep in my gut that he was alright.

"No, it worked. I'm sure of it. As sure as I am that we're on the right track to finding Maria. My exact wish was to find her before she killed my mother. Maybe the universe is leading me up to the very moment before she draws the sword, or something."

I was grasping at straws but as I spoke the words, I felt them to be true.

"Perhaps," Finn agreed and nodded. "Christ, I didnae know the universe was so bloody literal."

We laughed as our carriage took a turn and I saw out the window that we neared The Siren's Call. The familiar rows of trees, now highlighted with tiny lanterns, lit the long and narrow drive to the main house. I felt like royalty as we circled around the fountain outside and stepped out onto the groomed dirt below. The front doors opened to the outside as two men in fancy suits stood to greet and welcome the guests. We stood and waited for the second carriage to pull up and I watched patiently as Gus emerged and then helped a stunning Lottie step out. Her foot touched the ground and a heap of dark blue silk flowed from her body. A white-gloved hand took Gus by the arm and they came to meet us by the fountain.

"Are you ready?" Lottie asked me.

"Yes, let's get this over with," I replied.

"Over with!" Finn exclaimed. "I dinnae know about the lot of ye, but I plan to enjoy every bit of it." He tipped his head toward me. "Somethin' ye should consider doin' yerself every now 'n then."

I rolled my eyes and took Henry by the arm and the five of us marched toward the opened doors, lured by the sound of cheerful music and the scent of delicious food. As I stepped over the threshold, I was met with a blanket of noise and festive décor. Rows of fresh green garland hung from the ceilings and candles lit every corner of every room we passed. People of all sorts filled the spaces and chatted with hands full of fizzing glasses and appetizers. We turned a corner to the main room where guests danced about to the music being played. Men with fiddles and mandolins stood on an elevated floor and happily played the festive tunes.

Gus took Lottie and the two swirled into the moving crowd as if they belonged there. Finn had already run off in search of food and drink. Henry and I circled around, tasting the tiny food that coasted by on large trays. Enjoying the festivities. Before long, Wallace found us and approached. Taking in the sight of me with an almost proud collection of thoughts. Her tall body was draped in dark green silk, white ruffles poking out around her wrists and neck. Her dark hair pulled up from her long neck.

"I see you managed to find suitable clothes," she said by way of greeting and then switched her gaze to Henry, completely ignoring me. "You look absolutely dashing."

"Thank you for inviting us. The Call has never looked so alive," he replied and then turned to me at his side. "Care to dance, milady?"

I caught Wallace's eyes flicker with malice at the slight snub that Henry had given her, and she turned on her heel, sifting through the crowd and away from us. I tried not to think of what the ripple effect that might cause down the road.

"Oh, the pirate king dances now, does he?" I asked him with light mockery. This was something I'd yet to witness and I took his hand, eager to discover something new about the man I loved.

Henry confidently led me to the middle of the crowd and then placed a large hand at the small of my back, pressing me tightly to his body. I glanced up at his gleaming face and my heart melted. With his other hand, he clasped mine and began to lead me around the room. I followed him in awe, stunned by the way this magnificent man could do everything with such ease. I wondered then, who'd taught him to dance.

Despite being surrounded by dozens of guests, it felt as if we were the only people in the room. The way Henry held me, the way his eyes never left mine. I couldn't wait to spend the rest of my life with this man. Nervous, my mouth opened to speak, to tell him of the treasure I held between my breasts but, once again, was interrupted by a giant Scot.

Finn yanked me by the arm and pulled me to him. "My turn!"

"Finn!" I called out in dispute.

But I quickly relaxed into a carefree mood as the foolish redhead twirled me about in a clumsy manner. Henry stood nearby, laughing at my expense as Finn stomped around and jerked my arm to and fro.

"Your dancing could use some finesse," I told him as I gripped his arms for dear life.

He rolled his big green eyes mockingly and twirled us further to the center of the room. "I'm sure it ain't the only thing about me that needs a bitta finesse."

"Whatever do you mean?" I asked playfully, and we exchanged a stifled laugh.

Finn calmed a bit, dropped the quick and jerky movements, and we coasted around in comfortable circles. I caught sight of Roselyn Wallace near the edge of the crowd and pretended like the presence of her striking beauty didn't affect me. But it did. And Finn noticed the change in my body.

"Ye got nuttin' to worry 'bout, ye know," he told me and stole a quick glance her way before coming back to me.

I feigned a nonchalant composure, smiling and nodding at fellow dancers we passed by. "I don't know what you're talking about."

"Aye, ye do," he said in a Scottish purr. "I sees the way ye looks at her. But I also sees the way Henry looks at *ye*. Roselyn Wallace cannae hold a candle to it, Captain. What they had, t'was a long time ago."

My breath caught in my throat and my heart pounded against the interior of my chest. My feet unable to move. I stared Finn square in the face.

"What do you mean?"

His blotchy Scottish skin flushed red with the realization of what he'd done, and panic filled his eyes. "Uh, I mean, I didnae —"

"Finnigan Artair, you tell me right now. Were Henry and Wallace together in the past?"

The words left a scorched trail as they burned in my mouth. Finn wouldn't answer and his grip on my body ceased. Why did Henry lie to me? I had asked him if there was anything I should know. If there were anything to worry about. I fought back hot tears.

Finn's face pleaded with me to remain calm and refrain from prying. "Dian —"

I moved closer to him and lowered my voice, hoping it would placate him enough to give me the answer I wanted. Because, clearly, I wasn't getting it from Henry. "We're they...did he...*love* her?"

Finn's jaw opened but no sound came out at first. "Ah, Lass, I dinnae know the answer to that. I swear it." But my friend saw the pain I was in and offered what he could. "'Twas many years ago. Before me time with him aboard The Devil's Heart. I only ken what Gus told me."

Shaking with anger, I wiped the wet skin under my eyes. "Which was?"

He sighed helplessly and then nodded. "Aye, they was together. A *long* time ago. Henry mustn't have been more than a young man, fresh off The Burning Ghost. But he didnae love the woman. Not enough to stay, anyway."

It should have made me feel better, his words should have given me that assurance I so desperately needed. But I felt worse. I was drowning in a pit of my own despair right there on the dance floor. It felt like all my insides were pouring out and everyone was watching.

"Breathe, Captain," Finn whispered and took me by the shoulders, demanding I meet his gaze. I did. I took a deep breath, in and out. "What are ye frettin' over? That's history. He was a different man then." I began to calm, the anger dissipating and dissolving throughout my body. Finn waited until my eyes focused on his and he smiled wide. "He's a better man *now*."

I stood straight. The dance was over, and people began to mingle into groups and find seats to rest their tired feet. Finn was right. What was I doing? What was wrong with me?

"I'm sorry," I told him. "I'm not sure what came over me. This damn baby, it's making me feel crazy sometimes."

"Aye," he churred happily, "just wait 'till the bugger is born. Then ye will have yer hands full."

I laughed, despite the tears that lingered in my eyes.

"Are ye alright?"

I nodded with all the assurance I could offer, then walked to the outer edge of the room as Finn left in search of more wine. I scanned the space for a tall, blonde pirate. But came up empty. Henry was nowhere to be found. Part of me was grateful he didn't witness my discreet breakdown on the dancefloor but another part, a bigger part, began to worry. My mind picked up the leftover pieces of panic that still flowed in my veins and lit a spark. My heart sped up as I turned and craned my neck in search of him. Down the hall. In and out of rooms. Nothing.

I went back toward the grand foyer and looked up to the second floor that loomed overhead, searching the balcony that encircled and looked down from above. My gaze trailed along the golden banister and it was there that I found him. His back to me. His front to someone else. I couldn't make out who it was, Henry's massive frame blocked my view, but I could tell from his body language that he was speaking to someone. Finally, he turned ever so slightly, still with his back to me, but enough to reveal who had his full attention in the privacy of upstairs.

Roselyn Wallace.

My blood scorched through my veins with anger as I watched her perfect brown fingers caress the sleeve of Henry's arm, the way her body moved closer, pressing out the air between them. She leaned in and wrapped her long arms around his neck and, for a split second I expected him to push her away. But he didn't. Instead, Henry, *my* Henry, happy accepted her embrace. I fought down the vomit that threatened to rise in my throat, but I lost the fight as I watched her pull free of their hold. Just enough to place a tender kiss at the corner of his mouth. What little I had in my stomach wretched from my body and I turned toward a massive floor vase by my side, heaving the contents into it. Sending gross echoes bouncing through the large space.

"Dianna!" I heard Henry shout from above.

I stood and wiped at my mouth as I shot a cold stare up at the both of them. He seemed confused at first and turned to a smug looking Wallace before glancing back down to me, realization smeared across his face. In a split second, he came sprinting around the open hallway above, heading for the stairs. He was coming to explain. I wouldn't give him the satisfaction.

I began to back away, unsure of what to do or where to go. I just knew I couldn't be anywhere near Henry right now. My heart squeezed in my chest and warm tears stained my face at the betrayal I'd just witnessed.

"Dianna, wait!" he called out desperately. But The Siren's Call was a large house and the space between us was vast.

"No! Don't you *dare*," I yelled at the man, my voice echoing through the huge foyer. With trembling fingers, I stuffed a hand in between my breasts and pulled out his mother's ring. "I knew it. I *knew* it! And, to think, the only thing I wanted this entire God damn day was to give you *this*!"

I threw it across the wide-open foyer where it pinged off the marble floor and rolled to Henry's feet. He stopped, shocked, and bent down to retrieve the ring. I continued to back away, quickly now, and watched as his eyes widened upon examining the piece of jewelry. He stood, frozen in shock or fear or...something else, I wasn't sure. Turning, I heard the sound of a voice calling to me, desperately, as I ran out the door and hopped in an empty carriage before ordering the driver to go with haste to The Kraken's Den. Away from The Siren's Call. Away from Henry and the pieces of my broken heart left sprawled on that cold, marble floor.

CHAPTER SEVEN

I remember flinging myself from the carriage once I saw the swinging wooden sign of The Kraken's Den in the distance. The whole way there, I rocked back and forth, willing myself to keep it together just until I got there. Until I could fall apart in the comforts and privacy of my own room. Alone.

Despite the way the modified corset protested against my ribs, I wrapped both arms tightly around my torso and begged my brain to shut off. The images flashed through my mind, hot and vivid. But in a whole new light. Not just the still-shots from the day, but the long-forgotten memories of the recent past. My life before all of this. How simple it was. I'd taken it for granted, the safety and assurances of the future, the conveniences and ease of life.

Then, my mind neared the moment I came back home for Dad's funeral and the fateful chain of events that had led me to the past. My present. I wondered then, if it were all a matter of coincidence...or was my life nothing more than a result of some divine providence? Destiny? If that were the case, then I shouldn't wish my time back. There was no point. I would have ended up in the very same position in life, lost in the past with a band of pirates, knocked-up, and feeling utterly alone.

I stormed up the wide and winding stairs of The Kraken's Den and burst through my room door. With great frustration and impatience, I ripped the stupid dress from my body in pieces. Screaming. Crying. Tearing at the fabric and cursing how hard it was to rid my body of it suffocating hold.

Finally, everything I wore laid in a heap on the floor and I slipped on a clean shift before diving into bed. Sitting up, I plucked out the pins in my hair and tossed them to the floor near the dress and my shoes. It felt good to let my long black hair fall around my body. It calmed me. Brought me back to The Queen; my hair blowing in the sea breeze as I placed a hand atop of my red tricorn hat to keep it from catching in the wind. I missed the food Lottie would make. I missed playing in the kitchen with her and the feel of utensils in my able hands, chopping and peeling earthy veggies.

My eyes closed, I leaned my head back against the dark headboard and inhaled deeply, remembering the smell of my bed. The one I shared with Henry. Our quarters that filled with sunshine all day and came to life with candlelight at night. When Henry and I would lay in bed and profess our love for one another in so many ways.

A single tear fell from my eye, but I wiped it away before others could follow. God, I'd give anything to forget this all happened. Then an idea formed in my mind, refusing to be swept away with irrationality. I still had one pearl. Stretching, I leaned over to my bedside table and pulled out a drawer that contained a small, locked box. I opened it and fingered around the contents until I found the pearl and pinched it between my fingers.

Yes, I told myself I'd save it and wish us all home in the end. But...what if I wished myself back to the future? Away from all this mess and the dangers of the past. Just leave it all behind and wipe my hands of everyone and everything I touched since washing up in 1707. My baby would be safer, that was for certain.

But would I be happy?

I knew the answer almost as fast as I asked the question. No. I'd be absolutely miserable living in an era in which I never did fit in. I'd be forced to look at the face of my child every day, forced to remember its father, my glorious pirate king and the misfit band of pirates I called friends. No, *family*. I could never leave them. I could never leave Henry, no matter what he'd done.

I put the pearl back and returned the box to its place next to my bed before I yanked the heavy quilts up around my neck and laid down to go to sleep. At first, I thought I'd never fall asleep. But within seconds, the weight of the day came crashing down and my eyes forced shut, spinning me into a deep, and dreamless rest.

It was sometime later when I awoke again. How long, I had no idea. But my head protested as I opened my eyes to the slight noise that woke me. Henry had entered the room and attempted to quietly shut the door behind him. I watched with one eye fully open as he turned and looked at me, his face sullen and defeated. Slack from drink. Swiftly, he removed his coat and slung it over a chair.

"You're awake?" he asked softly.

Not moving, I replied against the pillow, "I am now."

He sighed and slipped off the new black vest and white shirt, adding it to the pile in the chair. "I'm sorry to have awakened you. Although, I'm ashamed to admit I'm relieved you're not asleep."

"Why's that?"

He looked at me with an expression that begged understanding. "I was hoping to talk to you. That's...is that not what we do?"

Damn it. He was right. We'd made a pact, back aboard The Queen, to always be honest and talk our way through anything. It's how I helped him deal with the PTSD and the darkness which haunted him each day. It's how I got over what happened to me aboard The Black Soul. I talked it to death in the days following. Henry never wavered, never grew tired, and always accepted the way I felt about it all. How I cared for Benjamin, because he was my friend. How Pleeman gave his life to save mine and the guilt I carried back to shore. Henry helped me through it all.

I at least owed him the chance to speak.

Carefully and tiredly, I pulled myself up and leaned against the wooden headboard. "So, talk."

My eyes raked over his body and how the exposed skin of his chest moved over the lithe muscles. How it rose and fell with quick, nervous breaths. With empty palms upturned, he said, "I came to beg your forgiveness. I was a fool to withhold the details of my past with Roselyn. And I was cruel to let you think there was nothing to worry about."

I raised my eyebrows and folded my arms over my protruding belly.

"Christ," he spat in frustration and rubbed his forehead. "I'm still no good at this." Henry took two quick steps toward the bed then. "There *is* nothing for you to worry about. I swear. I just meant, I should have told you then and there. That I was once with Wallace. But that it means *nothing* today."

I chewed at my bottom lip as I let his sincere words sink in. I searched his face, void of any sign of deceit, and only saw a man riddled with guilt. Just not the kind I thought he should have. He didn't feel bad for betraying me, because he didn't. I could see that now.

With great willpower, I shifted over and pat the area on the bed next to me. "Come, sit."

Henry did as he was told, and took a seat next to me, his back to the door so he could face me head on.

"Dianna –"

"Tell me everything," I demanded.

"What do you mean?"

"You are everything to me. My life here in the past has no purpose without you." As I spoke the words, Henry's face became awash in confusion. "But I cannot be here if I'm left in the dark. I won't allow it. Open books, remember?"

He nodded.

"We promised. Never to withhold anything from one another." I paused and slipped my hand in his and Henry clenched tightly, desperately, as if he thought he'd never hold my hand again. "So, I need you to tell me everything about you, Roselyn Wallace, and how you're connected."

He seemed to accept that wholeheartedly but shook his head. "Don't you care to know what happened tonight?"

"I do. I mean, I will," I replied and recalculated my thoughts. "I want to know everything first. Then tell me what happened tonight."

Henry adjusted himself into a more comfortable position, kicking his boots onto the floor, but still held his grip around my fingers.

"It all started years ago." He guffawed. "Christ, so many years ago. It'd only been a few months after the witch and I cursed Maria and her ship. I was a free man. Careless. Gettin' into all sorts of trouble. That's when I found Wallace." Henry stopped and widened his dark eyes.

"Wallace Senior, I mean. Roselyn's father. He ran the port, colluded with both sides of the law, while also running a prestigious brothel. I went to him one day to pay the duty for the ship I was on. With the captain, of course. But Wallace took a particular interest in me. To this day, I'll never know what it was. But he chose me. Took me in, taught me the ins and outs of real piracy. How to do it and not get caught. How to work both sides. He put me on the path to get The Devil's Heart."

"So, how does Roselyn come into all this?" I asked.

"She's his daughter. An illegitimate child he had with one of the housemaids. But the mother died in childbirth and, for some reason, he kept Roselyn as his own."

"He must have been a decent man, then," I say.

Henry chortled. "Hardly. Wallace was a hard man. He ruled with an iron fist, and people feared him. No one dared miss a payment, or slight him in any way. He had nobility in his pocket and piracy wrapped around his finger. He raised Roselyn until she was a...ripe age, and then forced her to work in the brothel."

I gasped. "You can't be serious!" I did the rough math in my head. Roselyn seemed close to my age, younger, if anything. And if this was as many years ago as I'm told..."My God, she must not have been much older than –"

"Fourteen," Henry finished for me. "I was only a young man myself, but I knew that it was wrong. Profiting off his own daughter's body like that. It made me sick. So, I stayed. I let Wallace take me further under his wing. I got my ship, met Gus, built a crew, and worked for Wallace under the guise of a privateer. For years, he treated me like a son."

Henry halted, seeming unsure of what to say next. Or how to say it.

"He had no idea when Roselyn and I began to get...involved. At first, it was platonic. I pitied her for the vile things she had to do each day. But, the more I got to know the young woman growing up before my eyes, the more I fell for her."

"In love?" I asked, barely a croak of a whisper.

Henry shook his head and let out a deep breath, squeezing my hand. "No, not love. I cared for her, yes. But I always knew I could never love her. It just wasn't there." He touched the center of his chest where his heart would be. "I could feel it. So, I left as soon as I could."

I replayed his words over in my head, still unclear. "So, how did she come to own her father's entire business if he barely regarded her as his own heir to begin with?"

Henry grinned. "Like I said, Wallace regarded me akin to a son. When he fell ill, he wrote a will. Leaving it all to me. On the day of his passing, it was like the final piece of the iceberg breaking off. I could leave. I no longer needed him, nor he I. Roselyn was older, wiser, and more than capable. And the rightful heir to all, in my opinion. So, before anyone was the wiser, I did the paperwork and left it all to her."

We sat in silence for a while. Me, letting Henry's words stew in my brain. Him, waiting patiently for my forgiveness. Finally, as an act of progress, I squeezed his hand back and pulled him toward me, our faces just inches from one another. From this distance I could smell the stench of red wine and tobacco on his skin and inhaled it. It reminded me of when we first met and, I realized then, how he must have stopped shortly after. For me.

I pursed my lips and nodded. "Alright, so what happened tonight? Why did you disappear and why did I find you alone, with *her*?" My eyes glossed over. "Kissing."

"Oh, no. Christ, no. Dianna, we weren't kissing." He cleared his nervous throat as I raised my eyebrows, daring him to lie to me. "She had something to share with me. News. She's met someone and wanted to know if we'd all come to meet him. Roselyn thanked me for everything I'd done for her in the past, and apologized for her behavior the other day."

"That's all?" I ask.

"Yes, I swear it. The embrace you saw was just two old friends." Henry's head hung low. "The kiss, however, may have been slightly out of line."

I guffawed. "You think?"

"I assume she saw you down below and did it for a rise," he explained. "Roselyn was never one to shy away from a reaction. It was the only way she knew how to get her father's attention. I suppose old habits die hard. She's truly a good person, deep down. I promise you."

I tucked my knees closer to my chest, as much as my round belly would allow, and rested my chin atop them. Henry's hands rested around my ankles, desperate, waiting, pleading. I looked at the man before me and the sincerity in his black eyes. A range of hot emotions still flowed through my veins, but I was tired. And, in that moment, I wanted nothing more than for my pirate king to take me in his loving arms. To tell me everything was going to be alright.

"I believe you," I told him sternly, still holding my ground. "But this can never happen again."

His big black eyes pleaded with me from above my bent knees. "Y-you forgive me?"

I waited a beat before responding, softening my tone as I did. "Yes, I forgive you, Henry. I mean, there's hardly anything to forgive."

The relief that washed over him was palpable and Henry hugged into my knees. "Oh, thank God. I thought...I thought I was going to lose you."

I pulled at his head, now buried in the blankets that draped over my legs and forced his tear-filled gaze upward to me. I held his glorious face in my hands, rubbing the thumbs under the skin of his eyes. Much like he always did for me. Henry pushed a cheek into my palm before turning and leaving a kiss there.

"You will never lose me, do you understand?" I reassured the man and placed one of his hands over my belly. "I am yours and you are mine. Forever."

Henry smiled and twisted to fetch something from his trouser pocket. A ring. He pinched it between his fingers and held it out for me to see, both of us admiring its simple beauty and the promise it offered. The thin gold band and emerald gems held on by a golden claw gleamed in the dim candlelight of our room.

"Speaking of forever," he began. I tried to mask the sudden burst of sheer joy I felt rush through my body. But he saw it and his mouth widened knowingly. "However did you find this?"

"In the market today," I told him. "The ring caught my eye. Then Lottie pummelled the merchant into submission after he revealed the other goods he had." I laughed and shook my head. "Poor guy."

"Other goods?"

I leaned over and fetched the velvet bag from the floor next to us and dumped its content on to the bed. "That's what Lottie and I rushed back to tell you. Before we were hustled off to Wallace's. Maria's been around, long after reaching the shores. She traded these things just a few days ago."

"Christ..."

Henry's fingers moved over them, scooping up the ship-in-a-bottle I once gave him and smiled before discarding it in favor of his black leather journal. The piece that started it all. My heart broke for the boy contain within its pages. Funny how I would come to fall in love with the man who grew from it. I watched as he pried the pages open and rubbed his thumb over the dried blood stains. His mother's blood.

"My mother was a beautiful woman. She would have loved you dearly." The journal snapped shut and he tossed it on the bed before holding out the ring once more.

"And I know, without a doubt, that she would have wanted you to have her ring. *I* want you to have her ring. It belongs on your finger, and your heart belongs to me." He swallowed hard. "If you'll so willingly give it."

I shifted anxiously in my spot, moving my weight to my knees so I could fully embrace Henry in my arms, kissing his soft pink lips. "I already have. My heart's been yours since the moment we met. Maybe even before."

Happily, he stood from the bed and helped me follow. Henry then knelt on one knee at my feet and held the ring out in offering, smiling up at me.

"Dianna Cobham," he began, a slight waver in his voice. "Nothing would bring me more earthly pleasure than to have your hand in marriage. To spend the rest of my mortal life by your side. With this ring, I vow to hold your heart in my capable hands, to protect it, keep it warm, and always put it first. You are the shining light in my otherwise dark existence, and all I ask is that you let me stand in its radiance until we depart this world together."

With a deep breath, I wrung my trembling fingers through his messy blonde hair, smoothing it back from his face. "That's quite the vow," I said.

Henry took my hand and held the ring in his other, waiting. "A vow I do not make lightly. Dianna, will you be my wife?"

"Yes," I replied finally.

Quickly, Henry slipped the ring over my finger where it fit so perfectly and then joyously jumped to his feet. Two hands slipped under my arms and he lifted me in the air as we spun in a circle. I laughed loudly, giddy and drunk on the sudden burst of happiness as he set me down and took my mouth in a feverish kiss. Long, hard, and full of desire for me. Our warm lips pressed together as we hungrily drank each other in. Pulling and pawing at what was left of our clothes. I stepped back as Henry's anxious hands yanked the shift over my head, revealing my completely naked form.

"Take me, Henry," I told him, panting. "Make me forget the world exists."

His chest heaved with quick breaths and his arousal was evident in the space between us. My skin crawled with hot, prickly goosebumps as every fiber of my being ached for his hands on my body. For him to take me then and there and ravage me until there was nothing left but a spinning room and my trembling legs. His dark gaze pierced the air and he became the hungry with desire. A low moan erupted deep from within his body as he closed the distance between us, grabbing my hair in his fist and pulling my head back. His mouth hovered over mine.

"Gladly."

CHAPTER EIGHT

It's funny how an eternity of assurances still can't keep the anxiety at bay sometimes. Just hours ago, Henry had professed his love to me and asked to join our lives together. The ultimate act of true love. But, as I lay there in the early morning light that shone in through the tavern's window, my head nestled into the warm crook of Henry's arm, I fought with my mind. My worries. Concerned about our near future and what part Maria would play in it. Would I fail? Would my sister kill me instead?

When I managed to shake the crazy thoughts from my brain, the empty space filled with concerns for my baby. Would it be healthy? Would I carry it to term? What if there were complications during labor? What if I died in childbirth like so many women of this time did?

I couldn't bear the thought of leaving this world without being wed to Henry. I wanted our lives to be joined just as our hearts and souls were. I wanted to offer myself to him in the ultimate way. To stake my rightful claim.

We laid in bed, Henry still sleeping soundly, and I carefully twisted a ring from his finger; thick and silver with the shape of a skull carved into its face. I mindlessly slipped it down over each of my fingers, as I gazed across his bare chest out the brightly lit window, until it fit securely around my thumb.

I sucked in a deep breath in an attempt to calm my nerves, but the air struggled as I inhaled. In my arms, Henry stirred, waking from sleep. I craned my neck and watched in admiration as he wiped his tired eyes and yawned, the warmth of his glorious body escaping the blankets.

"Good morning," I said and kissed his chest.

His arm, wrapped around and under me, tightened. Pulling me closer. "Good morning, my queen."

"About that," I began and swallowed hard. "I think we should get married as soon as possible."

Henry shifted and turned on his side, facing me. "Is everything alright?"

"Yes," I told him, moving my still naked body close to his. "I just want to truly be your queen, and you my pirate king. I don't want to wait. I think we've done enough waiting for one lifetime. Don't you?"

"Yes, I can't argue with you there."

His searching fingers found my warm thighs and slid between them. My breath caught in my throat as he guided one of my legs to rest over his hip and my body shivered. His face nuzzled my neck, sucking and nibbling at the tender skin there.

"When do you propose we wed, then?" he asked between kisses.

My head tossed back in ecstasy and I fought to form words. "T-today?"

Henry came to a screeching halt and looked into my face. "*Today*?"

I rolled my hips, grinding our centers together. "I don't want to wait, remember?"

"Well, then," he replied with a pleasant grin and tugged at my leg. "I best make this swift. We've got a wedding to plan."

A long, blissful while later, we stood in the privacy of our room and helped one another dress. I buttoned his shirt as his fingers tightened the strings at my chest. My long red, cotton skirt fell heavily to the ground and threatened to catch underfoot with every step I took. I cursed the garment internally and prayed for the day this baby would leave my body and I could go back to wearing my beloved pants.

"Are you ready?" Henry asked me and took my hand in his.

"Yes," I told him with the utmost certainty.

We left the room and bound for the stairs, ready to gush to our friends the news and beg for their help in planning the shotgun wedding. Henry had pleaded with me to consider a church, to wear a white gown, and have all the expected things a normal wedding should. Insisted that I must want them. But I told him, again and again, that all I wanted was to be his wife. I didn't need fancy clothes or a stuffy church. Truthfully, the one thing I wanted most of all was to marry the love of my life on Newfoundland soil. But, since we were so far from the comforts of home, the next best thing would have to do.

Together, we stepped off the last stair and searched around the early morning crowd for our crew. Our friends. My eyes found the back of Lottie's blonde head and I made a b-line across the floor toward where she sat at a table with the rest of them.

"Good morning, everybody," I greeted, standing at the end of the narrow table. They all looked up from their food and regarded us curiously. "Henry and I have some news."

"Christ, it better be good news," Finn moaned. I saw then, the evidence of a severe hangover on all their faces and I felt bad for what I was about to ask of them. "Not sure we're fit t'handle a crisis this early in the marnin'."

I laughed and turned to Henry.

"No, I assure you Finnigan," Henry said. "It's good news. No crisis here. Except…" He gave the floor back to me, unsure how to proceed.

I held up my hand that sported the gorgeous emerald stone and waggled my fingers. "We're getting married." I pursed my lips in excitement and then added, "Today."

Their eyes widened, and Finn called out loudly.

"Aye, 'tis about time ye two did it!" he stood and came around the table, slapping Henry on the back before scooping me up in a clumsy embrace. "Congratulations, Lass."

I laughed and hugged him back. My friend. I loved him dearly. If it weren't for Finn and his protective ways, I may not have ever gotten the chance to get to know Captain Devil Eyed Barrett. He vouched for me when no one else would. Took me under his wing and made sure I had a place aboard The Devil's Heart. I owed him my life.

"I, um, I was hoping you'd give me away," I said by way of asking.

The giant Scot erupted with a massive chuckle. "You want the likes of me walkin' ye down the aisle?"

"Well, not an aisle," I told him. "We've decided to get married aboard the ship. It's the closest thing to home we all have, and I can't think of a better place to do it. It's been our home for so long."

Everyone seemed to approve of the idea and Finn's brightened face calmed with a sense of pride. "Of course, I'll walk ye down the aisle. It'd be me pleasure."

He released me back to the ground and Lottie took his place, wrapping her delicate arms around my neck and pulling me close. She whispered in my ear. "I'm so happy for you."

Lottie pulled away and we exchanged a tearful glance. I mouthed the words *'thank you'* and she sat back down. My friend tried to be discreet, but I caught the swift movement of her foot as it kicked Gus's leg underneath the table. He awkwardly cleared his throat and stood, shaking Henry's hand with a curt nod.

"Congratulations, both of you. This is excellent news." He stopped to adjust his wide leather belt. "So, what is it you need?"

"I'll need your help to find a local priest who can perform the ceremony on such short notice," Henry told his oldest friend, clasping him by the shoulder. "And I'd hoped you'd stand with me."

"I'd be honored," Gus replied and smiled, a genuine expression that actually reached his eyes.

My heart warmed at the exchange.

"Lottie, I'll need your help finding a dress." The image of my gorgeous evening gown lying in heaps and pieces upstairs flashed through my mind. "I, uh, just don't have anything suitable."

Her eyebrow arched, and she snickered. "Another trip to Madam Guthrie, then?"

I let out a small laugh and nodded. She would be the best choice. "Finn, can you round up the boys? Let them know? And perhaps get them to help clean up the deck?"

"Aye, aye, Captain!" Finn replied half mockingly. But I knew he'd get the job done.

***

With bellies full of hearty breakfasts, we all set out with our duties. Lottie and I took a carriage to Madam Guthrie's and entered the quirky clothing store. I wasn't in the least bit surprised to find her ready and waiting for us. As if the old woman knew we were coming.

"Ah, good morning, my lovely ladies," she greeted, sipping tea from a delicate piece of china. Today her wispy grey hair was twisted up with a white silk turban. "Did you enjoy the party last night?"

"It was wonderful," Lottie replied. "The food was excellent. And I may have drank a little too much wine. My body pays the price this morning."

Madam Guthrie let out a low cackle of laughter and set her tea down on a small, round table for a refill. She glanced up as her long bony fingers gripped the teapot. "Care for a cup of tea, ladies?"

"No, we're fine, thank you," I told her. "We're here for a dress."

"A dress?" she said with a guffaw. "I do believe I sent you on your way with a gorgeous garment just yesterday, did I not?" He eyes examined my face and teased me somehow, with the possibility of knowing. Knowing that the very dress she spoke of laid on the floor back at The Kraken's Den.

I felt the skin of my cheeks turn red. "It's, uh, not quite what I need for today."

"Oh? What sort of dress are you hoping to find, then?" She began slowly walking through the store, sipping her hot tea and adjusting things on shelves with her free hand.

"Something suitable to get married in?" I said by way of asking.

Madam Guthrie spun around, a sense of purpose splashed across her face, and she set down the teacup. "A wedding, you say?"

"Yes, can you help me?" I asked her, and side-eyed a quiet Lottie who stood dutifully next to me. "On short notice again? I'll pay you extra."

She shook her head and waved me off. "Nonsense. Dressing brides is one of my favorite things to do. I'd be honored." A pleased grin widened across her wrinkled face. "And I have just the thing."

"Wait!" I called after her as she scuttled through the many rows of clothing. "It can't be too fancy!"

"I know!" she called back from somewhere.

I chewed at my bottom lip. "And the wedding will be outside, so it can't be too thin!"

"Of course!" her voice rang back, further away now.

Unsure, I turned to Lottie, chewing at the nail of my thumb.

"See?" she said and raised her brow as the word *witch* mouthed silently.

I laughed with a sigh, brushing her off.

"Seriously," she said just above a whisper and nodded toward the little table with the teapot where two empty cups sat. Waiting. "She knew we were coming."

"Don't be ridiculous," I told her.

We heard the sound of Madam Guthrie shuffling her way back to the front of the shop then and we turned to meet her. The old woman emerged from the back of the store with a long, thin garment draped over her arms. The fabric seemed to be a mix of silk and some sort of sheer. It wasn't white, but a subtle grey. Like fog over the ocean, early in the morning. A light dusting of clear gems sprinkled down over the fabric, catching the sunlight like freshly fallen snow. I admired the way the waist cinched just under the breast, and the long sleeves it offered. But most of all, I loved that is didn't have a corset.

"Madam Guthrie," I said in total awe. "Wherever did you find something like this?" I knew it was out of place, not of this time. Women in the 1700s coveted their poufy dresses, heaps of fabric, and tightly packed corsets. This...this was something I would have wore in my time.

The woman gave me a cheeky grin. "I made it."

"What?" I said, confused.

"I had a vision for this dress, many years ago," she explained. "I knew no one would buy it but, still, my hands begged to create the cursed dress. I've held on to this ol' thing for nearly twenty-seven years. Just waiting for the perfect woman to grace me with her presence and wear it beautifully. You'll do just fine, I imagine."

I tried not to think of the odd timing. How this lady had the sudden creative urge to make such a dress as many years ago as I was old. It didn't make sense anyway. Unless time existed in a way we had no means of grasping. That the layers of our world weren't, in fact, neatly stacked and strung along in a train-like formation. Past, present, and the future. Perhaps...everything existed at once, in some form or another. Connected in an unearthly way. The future affecting the past just as much as our actions trickled into the days ahead.

I still stared at the dress in awe. "Well, it's...it's perfect," I said. "More than perfect. I'll take it."

"Let me guess," Lottie chimed in with a bratty grin. "No need to try it on? It's just the right fit?"

Madam Guthrie challenged her expression. "But of course. I wouldn't present it if I knew it wouldn't." She moved her hand under the fabric and it shimmered in the light. "It may be old, but I kept it well."

Lottie jut her jaw back and forth as she crossed her arms. "Uh huh, sure."

I flashed her a *be nice* look and she released her arms to fall at her sides as she smiled at Madam Guthrie. "I apologize, Madam. I meant no offense."

"Yes, you did," the old woman replied but Lottie's words only seemed to amuse her. "Think what you will of me —" she paused as she failed to hide a smirk, "Charlotte Roberts."

We gasped at the use of Lottie full name, a name we did not tell the shop owner.

Madam Guthrie shrugged nonchalantly, and her mouth turned down in a carefree way as she regarded Lottie up and down. "Perhaps I'm a witch. Perhaps not. But I *am* good at what I do. It's a gift not bestowed to others."

Lottie's cheeks turned crimson in embarrassment. "I really am sorry."

The woman turned and carefully lowered my wedding dress into an open box just big enough to fit it. "That's quite alright, dearie. Just be sure to come back to me when your wedding day comes."

Lottie laughed and shook her head. "Oh, no. I'm not –"

Madam Guthrie placed a wrinkled hand over Lottie's arm and peered up at her from the tiny spectacles that balanced on her nose. "I have just the dress for you."

It was a show of acceptance to Lottie's apology. But what else could my careless friend do but smile and nod? She knew as well as I did that, deep down, marriage was something she wanted. With Gus. But that was a story for another time. For today was *my* big day. I had a wedding to get ready for and the man of my dreams waiting for me.

CHAPTER NINE

After we left Madam Guthrie's, leaving my perfect gown in the capable hands of our driver, we piddled around in the lower section of Market Square. Lottie left me to go grab a few things she said she needed and I wandered through the smaller shop fronts, looking for something of my own. Henry needed a ring, too, and I was determined to find something that matched him as perfect as his mother's ring did me. I found a small merchant tent that sold an array of tiny objects. All forged from metals. Trinkets and tools, utensils and belt buckles.

"Your things are beautiful," I told the merchant. A tall and lanky woman with messy red hair she attempted to tuck back into a bun.

"Thank ye," she replied kindly. "Me husband makes it all. He's a blacksmith."

"Do you happen to have a ring?" I asked her. "Fit for a man?"

"Rings?" She looked puzzled.

"Yes, I'm getting married and my husband to be needs something that can keep up with his...lifestyle." The corner of my mouth twitched with the hint of a grin, thinking of Henry swinging a sword against the kraken. Climbing the side of the ship. His strong hands flinging thick ropes. He needed a piece of jewelry fit for a titan.

The merchant lady appeared hopeless as she searched over the table of hand-forged items. "Nae, Miss. I'm sorry, but I dinnae have a ring suitable fer a weddin'."

Disappointed, I gave her a friendly smile and nod before turning away.

"Wait! Miss!" she called after me.

I spun on my heels and took the few steps back to her table.

Candace Osmond

"I dinnae have a fancy ring," she began and then pulled a small jewelry box up from underneath the table. "But I do have these. Mismatched trinkets, jewelry with flaws that none buy. I dinnae ken if anythin' will work but yer more than welcome t'have a look. Take whatever ye wants. It's of no value t'me."

"Really?" I asked, beyond grateful.

She nodded happily and pushed the box toward me. I fingered through its tiny contents; an array of napkin rings, keys, buttons, and belt buckles, until a thick iron loop fell over the tip of one of my fingers. I plucked it from the wooden box, noting the simplicity of it. The way the blacksmith opted for squared edges instead of round which created a wide surface to carve a tiny Celtic trinity knot. The symbol for internal life. To make sure, I slipped it over my thumb and smiled at how it fit so right.

"I'll take this one," I told the woman and she didn't bother to hide her sense of surprise. I found the most perfect ring to give Henry in a box of her discarded goods. Items she never would have sold or had on display. To her, it may have been getting rid of something useless, but it was priceless to me. I'd never be able to repay her for the value it held for me.

"Are ye sure, Miss?"

"Yes." I nodded and glanced at the box again. I knew how I could repay the kindness. "I'll take the whole lot, actually. I insist on paying for it. How much?"

After some more looking around, I met with Lottie and we headed back to The Kraken's Den. The sun was bright and warmed the frosty air, but a sprinkle of light snow still trickled from the sky. It was magical. I couldn't hide the sheer joy that seeped from my pores. I could feel it. Splashing across my face and running down over my skin.

I was marrying Henry today.

"Are you nervous?" Lottie asked me, her hands gripping something wrapped heavily in cloth.

I didn't even need to think about it. "No, not at all. It's the only thing in my life right now that I can be so sure of."

"You're going to make Henry faint when he sees you in that dress." She threw me a quick wink and glanced out the window. We were nearing the Den.

I laughed. "God, I hope so. That's the whole point, isn't it?"

She quirked an eyebrow. "Among other things, I imagine."

The carriage filled with girlish giggles as we came to a full stop and Cillian opened the door to let us out. I emerged to the street below, after Lottie, and turned back to our driver.

"Can you see to it that this is delivered to The Siren's Call?" I asked as I handed him a letter I'd written while at the market. Addressed to Roselyn Wallace.

He took it without question and slipped it inside his jacket. "Of course, milady. Will there be anything else today?"

"No, thank you, Cillian." I gave him a polite nod. "You've been wonderful."

He tipped his flat cap. "I wish you all the best on your wedding day, milady."

The docks were empty of the usual crowd that bustled about the ships. The late afternoon sun shone down from above and warmed the tiny snowflakes that threatened to fall, resulting in a beautiful sprinkle but nothing on the ground. As if the universe saw fit to provide the most beautiful and delicate backdrop to my wedding day. I held the dress box in my hands and cast my face to the skies, smiling as the cool flakes kissed my skin.

Lottie and I walked toward the plank that led to The Queen. A rush of warmth spread over my body at the sight of her tall masts piercing the air, the cream-colored sails tucked back neatly. The bright red and gold paint, although now worn and patched from damage, flashed through the rows of black and browns. My Queen, my home. Gus waited at the plank, dressed in the formal wear from last night, his scraggly brown curls swept back in at the bottom of his neck.

"Hello, Gus," I greeted happily.

He took the box from my hands and tucked it under an arm while his other hand reached and helped me step across. "Fine afternoon for a weddin', don'tchya think?"

I smiled and grabbed the thin rope that lined the sides, trying to contain my excitement. "It is."

My foot touched the deck of my ship and a strange calmness washed over me. That sense of returning home. Henry was right to choose The Queen for the ceremony. I heard Gus and Lottie embrace and whisper to each other behind me as I searched the surface of my ship. They'd done an excellent job at repairing the damage and cleaning her up. Almost as good as new. If I didn't know where to look, if I didn't see the damage happen with my own eyes, I wouldn't have been able to tell.

But the yellow paint, brighter in some areas than others, the new boards, straighter and stiffer than most held the tell-tale signs. The map of our grand adventures and near-death experiences. Today would add a layer of joy and happiness, though. A new adventure. A new memory that the ship would forever carry. Finn's heavy leather boots stomps across the deck toward me and I turned my attention to him, taking in the sight of the giant Scot clad in his traditional garb; the kilt I got for him, the pressed coat as green as his emerald eyes and lined with gold buttons.

"Good afternoon, milady," he greeted and bowed mockingly.

I laughed and pushed at his shoulder. "You fool." He stood straight and his eyes gleamed with pride, making my heart melt for the friendship we shared. I wrapped my arms tightly around his massive torso, barely able to touch them behind his back. "I love you."

"Aye, I loves ye, too," he replied in a whisper in my ear and then sniffled away the tears that threatened his manhood. "I had the boys bring aboard yer chests. Henry's down in me quarters belowdecks, gettin' ready."

"Excellent," I told him and pulled away of our embrace. "You've done a fine job getting the ship cleaned up. Thank you, Finn."

"'Twas mostly the boys, Captain. Ye should thank them."

He moved aside, and I saw Charlie, John, and Seamus walking by with wooden crates in their hands, heading toward the bow. I caught Charlie's gaze and motioned him over. He set the crate down, a jangle of glass objects rang through the air and he ran over to me, smiling wide.

"Thank you for the wonderful job you did on the ship," I told him sincerely. "With the repairs and cleaning it up today. I really appreciate it."

Still hesitant to use his hoarse voice in front of me, the boy only nodded and tipped his cap before running back to his friends to finish the task they'd been doing.

"Aye, best git ye inside before Henry comes up," Finn suggested. "Idn't bad luck or somethin'?"

"I suppose. If you're superstitious," I replied and craned my neck to where Lottie stood with Gus, nodding toward my quarters.

Finn leaned into me. "After everythin' I've seen, I wouldn't be testin' it. Best play nice with the universe today, Lass."

He patted me on the shoulder and then ushered us toward my quarters. I bid my friend farewell as Lottie and I entered the room and shut the door behind us. I inhaled deeply the comforting smell of my room, realizing how I missed it so. The distinct tinge of mine and Henry's natural scent mixed with red wine, and musty books. I made a b-line for my bed, my fortress nestled in the crook of a wooden surround.

"No time for sleep," Lottie said. "We've got to get you ready."

I sat up. "I know, I just missed my bed."

She set our boxes and bags down on the small table. "I know, I miss mine as well."

It was a simple statement but carried in it a sense of something else. Worry? No. Impatience, maybe. I wanted us to get back home to Newfoundland just as much as my crew, surely. But we had a mission. I had to wait for my wish to lead me to her. But, I realized then, the way Lottie refused to meet my eyes, she feared that day would never happen.

I frowned. "Does the rest of the crew think that?"

"Think what?" she asked innocently and lifted my dress from its box to unfold it.

I tilted my head to the side. "Come on, don't lie to me." She stopped and finally looked in my eyes. "You guys are worried we'll never find Maria, right?"

"Let's not talk of it today."

"Please," I begged.

Lottie sucked in a deep breath and stuck a hand on one hip. "Well, you have to admit, Dianna. It doesn't look promising."

"But I made the wish."

"And what good of it?" she argued quietly. "We're no closer now than we were before."

"But we are," I replied and stood to walk closer to her. "Something pushed me to that merchant. Something made me look in the right direction at the right time to see Henry's ring. We learned that Maria has been hanging around. Somewhere close by."

She didn't look convinced.

"Look, like I told the boys, my exact wish was to find Maria Cobham before she kills my mother. That could mean the exact moment before she draws a sword or fires a pistol."

Her deep blue eyes flitted to mine. "What if Maria never finds your mother? What of it then? Will we wait here, far from home, for years? Just waiting for a moment that will never happen?"

I had no proper response, because I never considered that option.

"You should have been more specific with your wish."

"And say what?" I asked her helplessly. "To end her life? None of us need that blood on our hands. And how would we know, *truly* know that it worked?" A strange sense of rage began to fill my body and I felt my face warm. "No. I will find my sister. I will take her body in my own hands and ensure she gets the life sentence fit for the devil herself. If that's death by hanging, then so be it. But it will be by the hands of the law. It will be *right*. I will witness it with my own eyes and live the rest of my life free of that burden."

Lottie chewed at her lip and tapped fingers against the fabric on her hip.

"Just trust me," I said. "It's working."

She threw her hands up and shook her head. "I trust you, Dianna. I do. If you say it's working, then who am I to argue otherwise?"

I slid my fingers over her arm, pulling her attention back to me. "It is."

My friend's shoulders relaxed, and her eyes slowly shut as she nodded. "Alright."

Before long, a comfortable silence filled the room as we began to get ready. The only sounds were that of heavy fabrics rustling and drawstrings pulling taut. Hard bottom shoes clicking against the floorboards. Lottie wore the sapphire gown, looking like a queen of the sea. Her long blonde waves cascading down around her arms as her hands worked to pin the locks back.

"No, don't," I said suddenly. She stopped and turned to me, curious. "Leave it down. You're not a proper lady, you're a pirate and this is a pirate wedding. You don't have to pretend to be someone you're not. Not today. Not for me."

She hesitated but then smiled and pulled the few pins from her hair, letting it fall back to where it was. I watched as she took steps toward where her trunk lay on the floor near the door and opened it, fetching something from inside. She pulled out a small flat box, about the size of a shoebox, and handed it to me.

"I picked this up in the Square today," she said. I opened the lid. "I just thought...something fit for a queen. For the friend you've been to me. For giving me back the life I missed so much."

My breath caught in my throat at the item inside, a collection of twigs and white flowers, some sort of vine and crawling plant like an ivy. All formed into a large ring, the shape of a crown. It was beautiful, and the gesture tickled my heart. I looked to my friend with glossy eyes.

"Thank you." I lifted it from its box, held it up and placed it atop my head. "I don't know what to say, Lottie. It's...it's so perfect. Everything is." I had a quick wave of panic rush over me. "Almost too perfect."

Lottie's eyes widened, and she held me by the upper arms. "No, Dianna, look at me." I did as told. "Nothing is too perfect. This is a wonderful day, a day you deserve. You're just surrounded by people who love you. That's all. That feeling...it's not perfection. It's love. It's happiness in the face of all the darkness we chase."

She gently pushed me toward the floor length mirror, forcing me to look at the reflection as she stood behind and peeked over my shoulder. Our eyes met in the glass.

"You're marrying Henry today."

I took in a huge breath, allowing my lungs to inflate as much as possible before letting it out. My deep brown eyes raked over the form that stared back at me in the mirror. A beautiful woman. Black hair that spilled down over my upper body like silk. A dress so beautiful I could never have even dreamed it, the foggy grey fabric tucked under my breasts, hugging my curvy body and pooling on the wooden floor at my feet. I gently turned from side to side, the intricately sewn gems catching the late afternoon sun as my arms stretched under the long sleeves.

And a crown fit for a fairy queen atop my head.

With a smile so wide it stretched my cheeks, I repeated my friend's words, "I'm marrying Henry today."

Lottie placed a kiss on my cheek and then fled to the door where she poked her head out. I heard her ask someone if everything was ready and then shut the door before sprinting back to me.

"Are you ready?" she asked. "Finn is outside waiting for you."

"Yes, you go wait near the bow. I'll be out in a moment."

When she was gone, I remembered to grab Henry's iron ring and firmly secured it in my palm, the cold metal digging into my skin. I was nervous, but not for worry over what will happen. More of a nervous excitement to finally bond our lives together the way the universe so clearly wished them to be. Marrying this man, it felt...like I was following the invisible road that fate had laid out before me. As if all those years spent lost and alone, wandering through life with no purpose, just waiting for my flashing sign. Well, here it was, and I followed it wholeheartedly.

A knock came at the door, but it did not open. My signal to meet Finn, I suppose. I sucked in one last deep breath and pulled on the brass knob to find him waiting there, a cheeky grin smeared across his face. But it quickly morphed to expression of sheer awe as he took in the sight of me.

"Bloody Christ, I can see every bitta yer shape," he said under his breath. He stuck out his elbow and grinned madly. "Henry will likely fall to his knees. Ye looks like somethin' from the heavens, Lass."

"Thank you."

I looped my arm through his, my cheeks warm despite the cool December air. Madam Guthrie was right. The dress appeared thin, but its fabric gave me warmth. Or perhaps it was the quickness of my heart, beating faster and faster as we neared the front of my ship. The boys had lined the path with candlelight in glass jars which illuminated the snowy backdrop that now blocked out the sun.

I could see him then. Henry. My pirate king waiting for me near the bow, dressed in his new black vest and fancy trousers under the nice jacket I'd gotten for him. His long blonde hair had been neatly combed and tied with a black ribbon at the back of his neck. He looked so handsome.

And nervous.

I noticed the way his large hands wrought together anxiously, and his two feet discreetly shuffled in their place. As if he couldn't bear the burden of standing there in place as I slowly walked toward him. I met his dark, obsidian eyes, now covered in a film of gloss and beaming with pride. I couldn't help but match his expression and felt a single tear escape as Finn released me and I finally stood by his side. He reached and wiped at it with his thumb.

"Tears?" he said by way of asking.

I pressed my cheek into his open palm. "Tears of joy. I promise."

"You look like a vision," he told me, deep and full of emotion.

"Well, you're no popper yourself."

Henry chuckled lightly and took my hand in his as we turned to face the waiting priest. I hadn't even noticed him, or anyone else until that moment. My mind only searched for Henry. I glanced over my shoulder to where a giddy Finn and three deckhands sat on wooden crates gleaming up at me. With Lottie and Gus flanking our sides, Henry nodded to the holy man to proceed.

The next few moments were a blur of words jumbled together with the sound of my heavily beating heart and blood rushing through my head. I repeated as prompted and Henry followed. But when the priest turned the floor to us, to profess our vows to one another, my mind cleared and the world around me came into focus. It was his turn first.

"Dianna," he began, both his hands holding mine between us. "My life...it has been nothing but a series of cold and dark places. I felt trapped. I felt lost. As if I didn't even exist. And, for a time, I even wished I didn't."

He paused to choke down the emotions that threatened to escape his throat and I squeezed his hands.

"But then, by some divine force, the universe saw fit to throw you in my path. To make me love you. To show me I was worthy of being loved in return. I said it before, and I'll say it forever. Everything I am begins and ends with you. You are my light in the darkness. And I vow, on this day, to always protect your flame. To cherish it with my soul and keep it warm with my heart. I love you, Dianna Cobham."

The resound of tears being shed and sniffed away masked my own and I struggled to find my voice under the bubbles that had formed in my throat. I pulled one hand free of his to wipe at my nose and he chuckled under his breath.

"Uh, well, that's a tough act to follow," I croaked, and a wave of laughter erupted around us. I returned my hand to his and called my heart to speak. "Henry William White. You say I'm the bright light in your darkness, but I've always thought you were the force that broke through my empty world. Spilled into it like the ocean that once crashed through my home. I-I harbored so much hate for the world around me until you chased it all away."

I had to stop, to catch my breath, and Henry's chest heaved with anticipation.

"O-our lives, by some inexplicable fate had been woven together before we even met. That much I know to be true. And like a golden thread, your soul had been tethered to mine and it pulled me in. Dragging me home. There's no doubt in my mind that I was born to love you. And what I've learned is that we're both worthy of it. Today, I happily hand over my heart, my light, for you to have. To live in the protection of your darkness and sit by the fire of your love. Until we depart this world together."

"Blood Christ!" Finn bellowed from behind. "Yer makin' me bawl like a damn baby. Just git on with it, will ye!"

"Finnigan," Henry said boldly and shot him a look under his authoritative brow.

Finn cleared his throat and shifted in his seat. "Uh, apologies, Captain. Uh, Sir."

A few more words were spoken by the holy man before us and then Henry returned his mother's ring to my finger where it would stay forever. Shakily, I slipped the one I'd gotten for him over his ring finger. I breathed a sigh of relief that it fit perfectly, and Henry held it up for himself to admire. He spoke no words but gave me a side glance that was full of curiosity.

"You may now kiss your bride," spoke the priest.

We turned to face one another and before I could even blink, Henry grabbed me in one swift movement, throwing me back into the cradle his arms provided and took my mouth in his. My hands, no longer trembling, reached up and smoothed the skin of his cheeks, pulling his scruffy face into mine so I could drink him in. I felt his arms shift and slide under me before Henry scooped me up completely and turned to our friends.

"We're married! Let us drink!"

Our modest circle of friends erupted into loud cheer, clapping and moving about. Under the blanket of merriment, Henry pressed his forehead to mine and whispered, "I am yours. I love you, Dianna White."

"And I you," I told him.

CHAPTER TEN

T he musicians played loud, beautiful music with fiddles and lutes as I sat around and watched my friends celebrate the events of the day. A couple of hours had passed since we returned to The Kraken's Den and Mister Cresley proved himself more than accommodating. We paid him for a meal and a few drinks to be passed around to our friends, but the lingering guests had joined in the dance and he'd been continuously feeding us plate after plate. Drink after drink. Happy to just be included in the fun.

My poor pregnant feet throbbed, so I sat comfortably at a nearby table, carefully sipping on a small glass of port that I had watered down. Finn, loud and merry, danced around in a drunken stupor, tossing his free arm over everyone he neared. Telling them how much he loved them. I snickered and tossed a bit of fresh bread in my mouth before turning my attention to Henry. Lottie had scooped him up for a dance and he pranced her around like a gentleman to the jig that played. The deckhands, my boys, sat nearby, drinking weak ale and stomping their feet to the beat of the music. Charlie caught my eye and stood before making his way across the room to sit by me. He pulled out a piece of paper and a lead and scribbled something down.

Happy?

"Yes," I told him and smiled. "Very. More than I could ever imagine."

He placed a hand over his heart and nodded, telling me he was happy for me, too. Then he scribbled again.

I have a present.

"For me?" I asked, and he beamed. "Charlie, you didn't have to get anything for me. That's silly."

But he waved me off and reached into his trouser pocket to pull out a tiny bag that closed tight with a drawstring. He placed it in my hand and I loosened the strings to dump the contents into my palm. It was a wooden bracelet. A beautiful, intricately shaped bangle with tiny stars burned along the outer surface. Inside, the words *Dianna & Henry* carved by hand.

"Oh, Charlie, this is beautiful," I told him sincerely. "Did you make it?"

He nodded and raised his boyish brow as he motioned to the gift in my hands, reaching for it. I let him have it and he placed it over my fingers, slipping the bracelet down over my hand where it sat comfortably around my wrist.

"Perfect fit," I said and kissed his cheek. "Thank you."

After Charlie bounced back to the crowd, Lottie came over and sat down in a huff of sweat and booze.

"Sorry for monopolizing Henry," she said. "He's just a much better dancer than Augustus."

I laughed. "Gus doesn't dance."

"Exactly." She leaned back on her elbows as she stared out to our friends and slug back another mouthful of ale. "I saw Charlie give you something."

I held out my wrist to show off the dainty wooden bracelet. "Isn't it sweet?"

Lottie took my wrist, turning it over in her hands. "Yes, he's quite the little man, isn't he? That kid adores you."

I sighed. "We've been through a lot. I owe him my life. A debt I could never repay."

"I think you're doing just fine by taking care of him, giving him a place aboard your ship," she replied. "Charlie's as happy as they come, don't worry." She took another big sip and wiped at her mouth. "I have something for you, as well."

"What? God, you guys. You don't have to –"

"Shush now, it's your wedding day. It's customary to be showered in gifts." Lottie reached over to the table next to us where her cloak and satchel hung from a chair and reached inside the bag, pulling out the item she procured from the market earlier. The one wrapped in fabric. She handed it to me.

"It's not a fancy homemade gift, but I saw it and thought of you."

Slowly, I unwound the plain fabric to reveal a book. Leather bound in a warm brown and tied together with thick strands of suede. I ran my fingers over its surface before cracking open the spine to peek inside to find blank pages.

"The stories you told me about Henry's journal, and then your mothers, I just thought you should have your own. To write down your thoughts, recipes." She shrugged. "Perhaps even our crazy adventures."

I shook my head. "Lottie, this is probably the most thoughtful gift I've ever been given. Thank you."

"Really?" she guffawed. "A book?"

"It's not about what it is," I assured her. "Its what it could be."

"Well, I'm glad you like it."

Just then, the front door of The Kraken's Den opened and the heavy snowfall that now fell in the night came flowing in. We all glanced over, like meerkats peaking their heads around. Some had no idea the person who stood before us, while others tried to mask the gasp which escaped from their mouths. Henry's face flashed to mine and he took a few long strides over to where I sat.

"I did not invite her, Dianna, I swear it," he said with worry.

"I know," I told him and turned my gaze toward Roselyn Wallace and recalling the letter I'd entrusted with Cillian earlier. "I did."

"What?" Henry's face became awash with disbelief and anger. "Why?"

"I second that," Lottie chimed in and gave me disapproving look.

I shrugged. "She cares for you, Henry. As I'm sure you do for her, or *did* once upon a time. You play a very big role in the life she's lived, and I think she deserves to say congratulations, to share your special day, don't you?"

Henry's face jumped back and forth between me and the woman from his past who waited in the entryway, unsure whether or not to come in. I smiled and waved her over.

"Are you sure?" he leaned down and whispered to me.

"Yes," I replied. "Now, greet your friend."

Roselynn stopped a couple of feet away and I almost regretted my decision at the sight of her stunning beauty. Damn, the woman had no parallel. No one I could compare her to in my mind that would even come close to sharing the natural beauty she held. But I bit back my jealousy and stood to meet her.

"Dianna," she said. "Thank you for inviting me. I believe a congratulations are in order. I trust your day was something magical, yes?"

"It was, indeed," Henry replied for me and stepped closer to my side. "A simple ceremony aboard our ship. Dianna was absolutely radiant." He beamed down at me.

"Still is," she replied and looked me up and down with those chocolatey eyes and cat-like gaze. "That dress is stunning."

"Thank you. It was made by Madam Guthrie." Suddenly, after feeling like a goddess all day, I felt self-conscious in my gorgeous gown. Like all of my flaws were showing. But I brushed it away.

Wallace let out a quick laugh, a single huff, almost in disbelief. "The witch?"

"I knew it!" Lottie called from my side.

I shushed my drunken friend. "You're not serious?" I turned my attention back to Wallace.

She shrugged. "Well, there are rumors —"

"Wallacccce!" Finn bellowed and yanked her by the arm, twirling the startled woman around and then dipping her. "Now here's a woman who knows how t'throw a party. What are ye doin' here, ye wench?"

Still suspended in Finn's arms, I expected Wallace to reply with anger but was surprised when she erupted into a fit of laughter and swat at Finn's arm to let her go. "You foolish man, on the drink again, are you?"

He threw his mug into the air and called out, "Aye, 'tis a celebration! Drinks are in order! Come, dance!"

"In a moment, alright?" she promised Finn as he did a clumsy jig back to the crowd. She turned back to us, laughing, but her expression morphed to something serious.

"I wasn't going to come," she began. "I didn't think it appropriate after the way things ended between us." She spoke the words to Henry but held my gaze as she did. The apology was for both of us. "I admit, seeing Henry after all these years...I had little control over my actions. But that's no excuse. You didn't deserve that,

Dianna. I should not have laid hands on your husband. And, for that, I'm very sorry. I hope you'll forgive me."

Her words were sincere, but something in her face, something that flitted across her expression didn't sit well with me. Almost like a warning. But for what? To watch out? That she'll swoop in and steal Henry out from under my nose if the thought pleases her? I couldn't put my finger on it, but something deep in my gut told me to watch my back.

I kept up the charade of niceties. "It's alright, Wallace. A simple misunderstanding. I think it's me who owes you an apology."

She twisted her brow in confusion. "Whatever for?"

I masked a sneer with a fluffy smile before Henry could see. "For vomiting in your vase. I hope it wasn't too much of a mess to clean up."

Her eye slightly twitched but Finn came running up from behind and grabbed the woman before she could respond. Soon, Wallace was taken by the crowd, passed a mug of ale, and Lottie ran to join in the fun. I was tired and fit for bed after the long day I'd had. But watching my friends, in that very moment, brought me more joy than anything. To see them having fun, free of worry over our mission. If even for a night. It suddenly made me realize that they'd be okay without me. Without us. If Henry and I survived this mess and truly fled to some quiet piece of land where we could be happy and raise our kids.

Henry sidled up next to me, his long arm draping over my shoulders as I rested my head against him. Happy. Content. We needed no exchange of words and I happily listened to the beat of his heart against my ear.

"Are you ready for bed?" he asked.

"No, we can stay if you want," I replied through a yawn. "Wallace just got here."

"I still don't understand why."

Another slight yawn. "I'll explain later, when my eyelids can stay open on their own."

I felt his body jiggle with a slight chuckle, one that formed deep in his chest. "Come," he said and moved to stand. "Let's go to bed."

I took his hand and that's the last I remember. At least, until I touched my hand to the linens of our bed. No walking, no stairs. I was beyond tired. My pregnant shape hunched over as I sat on the edge of the mattress. Henry's hands worked over my body to remove the thick clothing. My ankles, by no attempt of my own, flung up onto the bed and were tucked under the blankets.

Henry kissed my forehead. "Sleep."

One last shot of energy swam through my veins and my arms reached out for him, my fingers hooking the collar of his shirt. I pulled his lips to mine and clumsily kissed them.

"No, no sleep. What do you mean? We have to consummate our marriage." I grinned sleepily up at his face as he hovered above.

Henry's body lowered down next to me and took me in his arms as my mouth searched for his. I moaned against him. But he didn't advance, only held me gingerly and covered me with his warmth.

"Hush, sleep. There'll be time for that tomorrow."

I melted into his embrace, basking in it as my mind eased into an unforgiving slumber. My body, pregnant and exhausted, had reached its limit of shopping trips and weird witchy old ladies. Of jealous ex-girlfriends and the constant walking around this town. Today...I got married. I held that thought close as the darkness caved in and I fell into an abyss.

***

You know that feeling when you wake up in a tent in the dead of summer, the air wrenched from your lungs, the heat trapped within the tent slowly cooking you from the inside out. That's what it's like to wake up in a fire. A real, live house-on-fire.

I coughed hard, the smoke tearing the skin of my esophagus as I fell to my feet from the side of the bed. My legs weak, I crumpled to the floor. Down there, the smoke wasn't as thick, and I sucked in a deep breath of air as I realized where it was coming from. Under the door.

"H-Henry!" I called, my voice hoarse. But he didn't respond. I coughed and tugged at the blankets that hung down over the side. "Henry!"

I felt the mattress jostle with his startled movements and he jumped down to the floor. "What's going on?" he asked and grabbed my hands as he blinked the remaining sleep from his eyes. "A fire?"

"Yes, I think so." I coughed with every word, the smoke getting denser as it seeped into the room.

"We need to get out of here."

He grabbed a piece of loose clothing from the floor and wrapped around the bottom half of my face before pulling me by the hands toward the door. He flung it open and a burst of flames shot through the hallway. The stairway just outside the room was collapsing, and we were trapped. Panic pushed harder, and harder through my body and I cried for the baby inside me. But Henry wouldn't give up.

"This way!" he yelled over the noise of billowing flames and cracking wood.

We went to the other side of the room, to the window, and Henry heaved it open. I gasped for the slight bit of fresh air that seeped in, but it was gone in an instant. He poked his head out and searched the ground below.

"It kills me, but I'm going to jump first," he told me.

"Yes! Go!" I told him, only considering his life. To put him before myself.

"Only so I can catch you!" he called to me, even though I was at his side. "You must jump, Dianna. You swear?"

I nodded.

"Dianna!"

"Yes! I swear, I'll jump. Just go!"

Like a wild animal, Henry grabbed hold of the sill and slipped through the window with such ease. I immediately went to the opening and peered down, hoping he was alright. He stood on the ground, arms stretched up and open. Waiting to catch me.

"Jump, Dianna! I swear to catch you!"

It was only one story. I knew I could do it with as much ease as Henry. But now I carried a life inside me and I panicked at the thought of missing my aim and meeting the ground. My body smacking against the hard dirt alley behind The Kraken's Den.

"Dianna!" His voice was drenched is desperation and helplessness.

I promised.

So...I jumped. I had to trust that Henry would catch me. And when I felt the hard smack of his strong arms underneath my body, a relieved cry sprang from my throat and I wrapped my hands around his neck like a vice.

"Shh, it's okay," he said against my ear as I helplessly sobbed. "I've got you. I've got you."

With me still in his arms, Henry took quick strides out of the alley and around to the front of The Kraken's Den. I heard the cries of people in the street, howling through the early morning fog. And then the sound of my name.

"Jesus Christ!" Lottie yelled and ran toward us. "Is she alright?"

"Yes, she's fine. Just shook up," Henry replied and then set me down. "Dianna are you alright to stand?"

I hadn't even realized my eyes were clenched shut until then. I pried them open to see my friend, her alabaster face smudged with soot. My arms found her, and Lottie hugged me back.

"Where are the others?" I asked her.

"Helping to put the fire out," she replied and pointed to where the remainder of my crew, clad in nothing more than undergarments and shirtless torsos, tossed large wooden buckets of water at The Den.

But it did nothing.

Like the beast of its namesake, The Kraken's Den became tangled in flames and threatened to take the adjoining building. Tentacles of smoke wrapped in and out of windows as they smashed from the heat. A loud, thunderous boom shook the air as the second-floor ceiling finally gave way and collapsed. Mister Cresley nervously walked through the crowd of shaking guests as locals brought blankets to wrap them in. He seemed to be counting.

"Mister Cresley!" I called and ran toward him. "Is everyone accounted for?"

He appeared solemn. "Without my ledger, I'm not certain, but I believe everyone is here. He shook his head, seemingly disappointed in himself. "Perhaps I'll count again. I feel as if I'm off."

"What happened?" Henry asked him. "How did such a fire start?"

"No one knows," the sweet old man told us. "Often, it's a chimney fire." He glanced toward what remained of the brick stack on the side of the tavern. "But I don't think that's the case. We just had them cleaned. The source of the flames seemed to have come from upstairs."

Just then, something in the first-floor picture window caught my eye. A shadow. A movement that passed over the light of the flames inside. I strained to see, as well as hear for anyone inside. And then the shadow moved again, closer to the window. It was a person.

"There's still someone inside!" I called and pointed to the window. "Look! Near the front desk!"

"Oh, dear heavens," a trembling Mister Cresley said. He took a step toward the tavern, but Henry grabbed his arm, holding him back.

"Don't," he told the man. "I'll go. Stay with Dianna."

The innkeeper hesitated, but only for a moment. He knew that Henry, a strong, able-bodied young man was far more capable of getting in and out safer than he. But I wouldn't have it.

"No!" I screamed and gripped the sleeve of his shirt. He peered back at me over his shoulder. "Please! Don't leave me. Don't go in there. Y-you'll be killed."

With a deep sigh, Henry took me in his arms and kissed me quick and hard.

"I can't bear the thought of losing you again," I whispered.

"You won't," he assured me. "I'll come back."

Before I could answer, Henry was gone. My eyes, unblinking, followed his figure as it busted through the once beautiful front door and ran through the ground floor of The Kraken's Den. The floor above burned with an unceasing fire and I yelped as another chunk of the structure came crashing down. Lottie's arms found me, and we held each other tightly as her borrowed blanket covered us.

"Bloody Christ!" Finn churred, suddenly at my side. "Did I just see Henry run inside?"

"Yes," I replied and swallowed hard against my smoke burned throat. "There's someone still in there."

Just then, the picture window that faced the front of the tavern exploded with an ear-piercing crash, shards of hot glass spilling into the street. The crowd, like a wave, moved back and shielded themselves. Gus and our deckhands dove away and dropped the buckets as they ran over to where we stood, huddled together.

"It's no use," Gus said as he coughed into his hand. "It's beyond saving."

"Henry's still in there!" I yelled and broke free of the safe cover Lottie's blanket provided to run for the Den.

Finn yanked back on my arm. "Oh, no ye don't! I'll go." He looked to Gus. "Watch them."

And, again, I watched helplessly as one of the people I loved most in this world ran head-on into a building blazing with smoke and flame. I held my breath in wait, eyes scanning back and forth through what openings still remained. My heart beat wildly as my lungs burned with lack of air.

Suddenly, a form moved in my vision and a bulky black figure moved toward the opening of the front door. I struggled for air as I watched, waiting, hoping. The massive figure morphed with color and shape as it met the light of day which seeped through the smoke. Finally, it emerged, three bodies draped over one another, coughing and wrenching the smoke from their lungs and collapsed on the ground just as the last of the structure caved in. Mister Cresley swiftly moved to fetch an old woman from Finn's one arm. One more burst of flames shot up in the sky and smoke billowed up in dark grey poufs.

"Henry!" I called and dove for the man lying in the street. He was unrecognizable. Covered in black soot, half his blonde hair singed up to his ear, and unresponsive. I dropped to my knees beside him and pushed at his chest. But he didn't react. "Henry!"

I whipped my head up to find Finn on his knees, coughing. But he seemed alright. Our eyes met. Surely, mine full of the worry I felt fill my body.

"I-I have to...he's not breathing," I told him.

"Have to what?" His voice lowered so only I could hear. "Can you save him?"

"Yes," I replied, thinking of the reactions I'd get when people saw me perform CPR, a method unknown to this time. But I didn't care. I had to save Henry. "Just keep eyes off me, okay?"

Finn nodded dutifully and moved to kneel between me and the crowd, his massive frame surely covering me from their prying eyes. I tipped Henry's head back, chin up, and checked for any obstructions in his throat. None. My hands, shaking from the cold winter air and the adrenaline that coursed through my body, pumped his chest as my mind silently counted. My lips around his, and I forced air into his lungs. Pump. Breathe.

Pump. Breathe. I worked tirelessly on his body, refusing to give up. Tears streamed down my soot covered face, pooling at the corners of my dry mouth, the salt stinging the skin there.

I pumped his chest harder. "Henry, God damn it!" No response. "Please! You promised! Come back!"

"Lass," Finn called over his shoulder. "We best move. We're too close to the fire."

He gently took my arm, but I swat it away. "No! I'll save him. I *have* to save him."

The fire raged just a few meters away and I could feel the heat burning my skin. I clenched my fingers together in one massive fist and raised it above my head before bringing it down to Henry's chest in a final act of desperation.

"*Breathe*, Henry!"

His body jolted to life and my heart banged against the inside of its cage. I helped him sit up as he barked a continuous stream of coughs. His eyes, confused and concussed, stared up at me.

"Dianna?"

I couldn't form words, relief flooded my body and I wrapped my arms around the man. But he winced in pain and I pulled away to find that his shirt was gone. Had been burned way by the fire that scorched his skin. Reddened and charred flesh swelled on his upper chest by his shoulder.

"Oh, God, I'm so sorry," I said, still trembling.

Henry gripped my fingertips and coughed. "You have nothing to be sorry for. You…you saved me." Despite the agonizing pain, he managed a smile and muttered as he fell back to unconsciousness, "Again…"

"Captain," Finn said once more. "We must leave. Now."

My head shot up and glanced around at the onlookers. The faces ridden with disbelief at what they witnessed me do. Despite the cover of Finn's body, I'd created a scene and they all watched with a mix of horror and wonder.

Just then, a racing carriage pulled up, casting a cloud of dirt over us. The door swung opened and Roselyn Wallace poked her head out.

"Get in!" she called to us. We all hesitated, and my crew looked to me for an answer. "I can help him!"

"There's not enough room for all of us," I told the woman.

"That's fine, Dianna," Gus said as he came to my side. "Take Henry. I'll make sure the rest of us gets to The Siren's Call safely."

"Are you sure?" I pleaded.

"Yes! Now, go! Get out of here before the questions start." Gus and Finn helped Henry into the carriage and I jumped in behind him, turning to my friends and willing them to be safe before closing the door behind me. And we were off, bound toward The Siren's Call with a half dead Henry in my arms and my world turned upside down.

CHAPTER ELEVEN

I sat by Henry's bed, in some random guest room at The Siren's Call as he slept. Wallace had sent for a doctor who had come with haste to clean and wrap Henry's burns. Finn and Gus, my brave men, had checked in and then headed back to the docks, to our ship where our trunks had thankfully been left behind after the wedding. At least we hadn't lost everything, which is more than I can say for poor Mister Cresley. I made a mental note to find him after this was settled and offer our help to rebuild The Kraken's Den. Lord knows we had more than enough money to build ten taverns.

"Dianna?" Wallace spoke from the doorway. I lifted my head from the side of the bed. "They're back with the trunks. You should come and get cleaned up. Get out of those clothes."

The woman seemed sincere. No malice or deceit hidden in her tone, and I began to rethink my view on Roselyn Wallace altogether. I knew she harbored feelings for Henry, but that didn't make her a bad person. And he'd told me she'd met someone. That she was happy and had moved on. I was reluctant to believe it. But now I wanted to give her the benefit of a doubt.

"Thank you," I told her. "For everything."

"It's no trouble at all, really," she replied. "Not for an old friend, anyway. I had slept at The Den last night, and had been on my way home this morning when my driver glanced back and spotted the smoke in the distance. I rushed back as fast as I could."

I stood and walked toward the door where she waited.

"You should let my doctor have a look at you," she added. "And the baby."

I wanted to decline the offer, she'd already done enough saving us from the street and tending to Henry's wounds so quickly. But I did worry for the baby. I'd inhaled so much smoke. And then the fall from the window. Henry had caught me, but my body met his a little too hard.

I rubbed a hand over my belly. "Sure, that would be…that's very kind of you."

She brushed off my words. "Please, no need."

"I insist. I can't repay you enough for your kin –"

"No." Her brown eyes flashed with impatience. "Please. I don't…it's the least I can do."

I gave her no reply. I left it alone and followed her through The Siren's Call, an awkward silence holding us together. Exhausted, I fetched some things from my chest and went to soak in a warm tub. As the layers of caked soot and smell of singed hair leeched from my pores into the water, I cried into my wet hands. Not tears of sadness but cries of relief. Of the adrenaline leaving my body. The events of the morning came rushing back and I realized how close we'd come to death today. If I hadn't woken when I did. If Henry's quick thinking didn't get us out of the building before it came crashing down around us. And then his unresponsive body lying limp in the streets. My heart squeezed.

With great effort, I got up in the tub and stepped out, careful of my wet feet on the slick floor. I dressed in a simple grey skirt and white blouse, refusing to even attempt to strap my massively pregnant body into a corset. What was the point? I tucked the loose ends of my blouse into the long skirt and hoisted the waist up over my belly before venturing out the massive house in search of my friends.

I found them, in Wallace's office, the room where I once draped over a chaise after nearly fainting. Gus, Finn, Lottie and our three young deckhands. All freshly clean but heavy with defeat and exhaustion.

"Dianna," Wallace said by way of greeting. "Come in and sit down. I was just inviting your crew to stay here at The Call for as long as they may need. That invitation, of course, extends to you and Henry."

"Oh, thank you," I told her. "But there's really no need. I don't want to put you out. We'll find another tavern once Henry is feeling better."

Her brow raised in challenge. "I have more than enough room to accommodate all of you. And the medical means to tend to Henry's wounds." She glanced at my stomach. "Not to mention you and the baby. You're far along, Dianna. You need medical care."

With a sigh, I glanced around at my friends, their faces drooping with fatigue, and I nodded. "Okay, we'll stay."

"Excellent," she replied and stood from her desk. "My doctor is ready and waiting for you in the room Henry's in."

I followed Wallace back to the room where Henry lay in bed, awake now. He tried to sit up at the sight of me, but winced in pain, forcing himself back into the bed. I ran to his side, slipping a hand into his.

"Dianna," he said in a raspy whisper. "Are you alright?"

"Yes," I assured him and forced a smile. "Nothing a good bath didn't help. How are you feeling?"

"Like a burnt roast," he replied jokingly and then cringed as he glanced down at his own chest, wrapped in white dressings.

"Are you in pain?"

Henry's hand squeezed mine. "Don't you worry about me. Was that old woman alright?"

"The one you pulled from the fire?" I confirmed. "She was fine. A few burns. But she's alive thanks to you and Finn."

He closed his eyes and pressed his head back into the pillow behind it.

"Don't you *ever* do anything that stupid ever again, do you understand?" I demanded.

Henry's eyes opened and gleamed up at me. "Yes, ma'am."

A single tear slipped down my cheek and I leaned over to place a gentle kiss on his lips before speaking softly against them. "I can't bear to lose you again."

"You won't," he mouthed against my trembling lips.

Behind us, Wallace cleared her throat. I'd forgotten she was even in the room. I pulled free of Henry and looked over my shoulder.

"The doctor is here to examine you, Dianna," she said and motioned to the single cot that sat on the other side of the large guest room.

As I laid in the tiny bed, letting the strange man run his cold fingers over my pregnant body, I stared at the ceiling and dreamed of home. Of the open meadows and the crash of waves in the distance. Of warm tea as the sun set on the horizon. But, I realized, after a moment's thought, it wasn't a Newfoundland of now. It was the home I came from. The one that wouldn't exist for another three hundred years, and the realization stunned me.

"There's not much movement," the doctor pointed out and pulled me from my daydream.

"What do you mean?" I asked. "Is that bad?"

"It can be," he replied, his wrinkled face worn with years of a stressful occupation. He stuffed some tools back into a large leather bag. "In this case, I think you'll be just fine with some rest. The baby is slightly distressed. Could be from the fire. Could be from lack of proper sleep and food."

"Well, I'm eating just fine," I told the doctor. "But I have been very tired. All the time."

He patted my hand. "Then I suggest you stay in bed, get some sleep. Don't do anything too strenuous. Listen to your body." He quirked an eyebrow and grinned. "And your doctor."

I thought of all we had to do, how we'd yet to track down my sister and that our mission had barely begun. My crew would need me soon. I couldn't just leave them with the burden of it all. Although, I know they'd do it in a heartbeat. But I'd pulled us along on this ridiculous journey of stopping Maria Cobham and I wouldn't stop.

I promised the good doctor to get some rest, and I would. For now. He left, followed by Wallace, and I laid there, holding Henry's gaze from across the room as we each yearned to be next to one other.

"The baby is fine," I assured him. "The doctor is just taking extra precautions. I can feel it moving around as we speak. Nothing feels different. Don't worry, alright?"

Henry's mouth widened. "If you say so." He tried to shift, to find a comfier position in the bed and winced again. He was clearly in more pain than he let on. "I wish I could lay with you."

Carefully, I pulled myself from my cot and darted for Henry, slipping in next to him. Mindful of his wounds. My lips found his and I placed a gentle kiss there before we both dozed off into a comfortable sleep, the glaring sun of the afternoon pouring in and casting a warm blanket over us.

***

The fog-like haze which surrounded my vision told me it was a dream. But, still, my body coursed with fear and panic at the sight of her. Of my sister, her hair as black as mine blowing in the wind. She turned to face me, her leather boots dangerously close to the edge of the cliff on which we stood. Her dark, soulless eyes held mine and her crooked mouth twisted into a sick grin as one boot stepped back, toward the edge.

"No!" I called after my sibling. I wouldn't let Maria take her own life. That was a right I had claimed for myself. To take her life in my hands and hand it over to the authorities where she would then suffer out the rest of her years rotting in a cell somewhere for all the horrible things she's done.

But it was too late. Before my arms could reach, she took one more step and flung herself from the giant windblown cliff. I ran to the edge in a fit of desperation and dropped to the ground to peer over to the abyss below. There was no sign of her body. I stood, speechless and slow from the tendrils of the dream, only to be met with Maria. Face to face. Her breath hot and heavy on my skin.

"Come and find me, sister. I'm right here," she said and then gave one mighty shove at my chest, sending me flying over the cliff I'd witnessed her fall from only moments before.

I awoke with a start, as if falling back into my own body, and sat up in a cold sweat. Clawing at my chest, gasping for air. A sleeping Henry lay by my side, unaware of the soul-shattering nightmare I'd just been thrown out of. I knew it was a dream, but I could still feel the warmth of my sister's breath on my skin. I shivered and quietly removed myself from the bed. The sun had gone down and our room had filled with the light of the December moon.

I crept down the hallway toward the room where I had bathed, where I left my trunk. I wanted to fetch my satchel and get some Advil for Henry's pain. Something I couldn't have done with the prying eyes of the doctor and Wallace watching over me.

I wandered the empty halls. Past tables taken over by massive flower arrangements, giant floor vases and stone statues. Paintings that loomed overhead with eyes that seemed to follow me every which way. The sticky echoes of my bare feet on the cold marble floors the only sound to be heard. After opening a few doors, slightly confused by the maze that was The Siren's Call, I found it, and looped the satchel full of futuristic goodies over my shoulder before heading back out to the house.

But I turned a corner and smacked right into someone. I tried to stifle the yelp that squeezed from my throat which became easier when I saw that it was Finn. The moonlight catching the fiery glimmer in his red beard and haphazard hair.

"Christ," he whispered loudly. "This place is like a damn maze."

"What are you doing up?" I asked him.

He quirked a brow. "I could ask ye the same."

I lifted the bag to show. "Needed my things. For Henry. He's in a lot of pain, he's just too stubborn to admit it."

He nodded in understanding. "I seen ya pass me room, the door was open. So, I followed ye."

"Couldn't sleep?" I pried as we walked the halls together.

"Nae, 'tis too quiet here," he said. "Like sleepin' in a bloody graveyard. I miss the sound of the sea beneath me arse."

I heaved a sigh and a cough followed, telling me the smoke hadn't yet cleared from my lungs. "I'm sorry, Finn. I know you're all itching to get back home. I am, too. I promise, I'm saving my last wish to get us there. Once we find Maria."

"Aye, 'bout that," he said hesitantly. "When do ye think that might be?"

We turned another corner and I spotted the familiar hallway in which Henry lay sleeping somewhere. I knew because it was the only hallway without a massive painting hanging on the wall. This one boasted mirrors around a giant bookshelf. I turned to my friend.

"Soon. Why? Do you doubt that we'll find her?"

He wouldn't look me in the eye, and I could see how he struggled to find the right words. For fear of making me mad or upset. "I just...we, the crew thinks that perhaps the wishes dinnae work."

"What?" I stopped in my tracks. "How could you think that?"

Finn shrugged. "How could we not?"

"No," I shook my head stubbornly, "The wishes worked. They had to. Because...if they didn't...that would mean Benjamin is still trapped aboard The Black Soul somewhere in the middle of the ocean, hidden away from the world." I took a deep breath, trying not to get too emotional. "Just waiting for me to break the curse. How long would a man hold on to that hope before losing his mind? I-I can't bear the thought."

Finn had no response because he knew I was right.

"No," I said again. "The wishes had to have worked."

He nodded, probably just to placate me, and patted my arm before taking a step back toward his room. "I believe ye, Captain. I just dinnae ken how much longer."

I watched my friend retreat to his room, his tall and broad figure disappearing into the shadows, and I fought back the urge to cry. I was an utter mess lately and I loathed being that way. I had to pull myself together, shake off the hormones, and get my head back in the game. I would find my damn sister. Soon. I just wish I had some sort of sign to assure me everything would be okay.

CHAPTER TWELVE

The next morning, after I cleaned myself up and dressed, I gave Henry some pain meds and a fresh dressing on his chest burns. The small tube of Polysporin I had wouldn't heal the extent of his wounds, but it would definitely help. I used it sparingly, knowing there'd no doubt be a need for it in the future.

I waited until the meds kicked in and he fell into a comfortable sleep before I slipped out in search of food. But also, in search of my crew. I was tired of waiting around, waiting for the universe to plop Maria into my hands and she sure wasn't going to turn up there at The Siren's Call. I had to get out there, walk the streets, ask questions. Maybe pay another visit to that merchant who traded with her for Henry's things. Anything, *any* little inkling that would steer me down the path to finding her.

I rounded one of many corners and stopped in front of a wide set of patio doors that led out to a grand garden of sleeping plants, covered in a thick blanket of snow. Everything was so white, so crisp. It was blinding. But I stared in awe at the still-beauty of winter before me. My eyes rolling over the curves and lumps of snow-covered benches. My stomach growled in protest at the delay of breakfast and I turned to leave the gorgeous view when something caught my eye. Something far out in the garden. Just like in my nightmare, her long curly black hair fell down around her shoulders, the cool breeze catching its waves as she slowly turned to face me. Those bottomless eyes sinking into me.

Maria.

A gasped as my hand took on a mind of its own and reached for the brass handle of the door. She was there. *Right* there. I could end this all right now and, as if bewitched, my body moved without prompting and turned the handle. But before I could haul the patio door open, a hand wrapped around my wrist and pulled me from the spell I was under.

"Dianna," Wallace spoke. "What are you doing? It's freezing out there and you don't even have so much as a sweater on."

I turned to her, blinking hard, my mind snapping back into focus, and shot my gaze back toward the garden in search of my sister. She was gone and there were no footsteps in the fresh snow. I shook my head. Was the stress of the failing mission making me crazy? Did I so desperately want to find Maria that my mind was manifesting images of her, both in and out of sleep?

"No, I-I -" Words evaded me. What could I possibly say to this woman? "I just wanted some fresh air. I'm feeling…a little queasy."

"You're just in need of some good food, is all," she told me with a smile. "Come, I had the cook prepare a morning feast for everyone."

"Oh, I can just grab something quick," I replied, still reeling from the hallucination.

She regarded me with a curious brow. "In a hurry to go somewhere?"

My eyes flitted to hers and I scrambled to mask the emotions I knew were washing over my face. "No. I mean, yes. I, uh, I have some things to tend to in town."

"Dianna," the woman said my name much the same way a disappointed mother would as her arms crossed over the tight-fitting red blouse. "The doctor said you should be resting. And eating. I see you doing neither of those things. What's your errand? I can have someone tend to it for you."

I tried to brush past Wallace, but she held an arm out in front of me. I mustered up the nerve to look her square in the face.

"I can manage," I told her stonily.

Her arm dropped and so did her polite demeanor. "Look," she began. "I know you and I won't ever be friends, but I'd at least like to try and be friendly."

I thought of her hands on Henry, her lips on his skin as I stared up from the floor below in utter horror. Like she was stealing away my very reason for living right in front of me. I thought of the way I just couldn't settle around her, no matter how nice she pretended to be. There was just something about the dark beauty that scratched at my nerves.

Wallace backed away, giving me space. "I think we can both agree that Henry is an amazing man."

I shrugged. "Of course. That's just a given."

She tipped her head to the side, the long chocolatey hair falling down around the front of her body. "And he would want you to take it easy, to listen to the doctor, Dianna."

"And I will," I said, trying not to grit my teeth at her pushiness. I dodged around her and began walking toward the smell of food.

"Then let me help you," she insisted.

I didn't bother to turn around. "You can't help."

"Try me," she called. "You'd be surprised what I can do."

The woman didn't let up and it bothered me to no end. Not just because I didn't want her help, but because I knew she couldn't. Not with this. But I spun around and walked back to where she stood in front of the glass doors.

"Thank you for the offer but there's nothing you can do unless you track down people who are hard to find."

Her expression turned curious. "I found you lot, didn't I?"

I guffawed. "Tracking down a crew of pirates at a local tavern isn't exactly stealthy."

Wallace seemed confused by my use of modern terms and I quickly amended before she had the chance to respond. "Anyone can find someone who isn't even hiding."

Wallace's hard bottom boots clicked against the marble floor underfoot as she crossed her arms. "And who, may I ask, are you trying so hard to find?"

I don't know why I said it, I don't know why I let the words spill across my lips, but they did. "Maria Cobham."

Wallace appeared taken aback and her dark skin turned a pallor green. "Why are you looking for *her*?"

I clucked my tongue. "See? I knew you couldn't help. Now, back off and let me do what I came here to do."

"Wait!" she called after me. I didn't turn back. "Wait! Dianna!" I heard her pace speed up from behind. "What if I told you I knew where to find her?"

I stopped in my tracks and spun around, unable to believe my ears. "W-what do you mean?"

"Like I said before, no one comes into my port without me knowing. They don't spend time in my town without me knowing their every move. Maria Cobham was here for nearly a week before she fled on horseback to the next town over."

My blood ran cold and icy goosebumps scoured over the surface of my skin. "Wait...you mean, she's not even here?"

"Here?" She appeared slightly panicked but then eased into understanding. "You mean, in Southampton?"

"Yes," I confirmed. "We have good reason to believe she's still hanging around here."

"No, Dear," she shook her head, "Maria Cobham would never stay put in a single place on land for too long. Especially not a place like Southampton where the list of warrants for her arrest far exceed any of the pirates before her."

I tried not to think of what that meant. That my dreams and hallucinations were just that. Nothing more than my tired mind playing tricks on me. I'd hoped that perhaps it was the wish, the universe telling me it was working, and I was heading down the right path. Regardless, I now had a lead.

"Thank you," I told Wallace and then took off in search of my crew.

"Where are you going?" she called after me.

"To find Maria Cobham!" I called back, unstopping as my feet moved with haste across the marble floor.

I finally found the dining hall. My friends were sitting around the end of the long, narrow table. A massive spread of delicious breakfast foods before them. They all glanced up and spotted me, huffing to catch my breath but grinning from ear to ear.

"I found her," I told them. "I know where Maria is."

Finn jumped up from his chair, the loud scuff of wood against stone floor screeching through the air. "Are ye sure? Where?"

"In the next town over. But she may not be there for long. We should go now," I instructed.

"That's a day's ride by saddle," Finn informed thoughtfully. "We could do it, just need some supplies first."

"Sure, sure," I said, barely hearing his words through the excitement that filled my brain. "Whatever we need, just get it together and we'll hit the road."

Lottie stood then and came over to where we stood in the wide doorway. "Dianna," she motioned to my stomach, "Are you sure you should be going? I mean, after what happened? The doctor said you need rest."

"No, I can rest once my sister has been caught," I told them. "I'm going."

"No, you are most certainly not," spoke a raspy, labored voice from behind.

I turned to find Henry, out of bed, bare-chested except for the bandages that wrapped around it. Out of breath from hurrying through the house. I spotted a guilty looking Roselyn Wallace at his side. She must had pulled him from bed when she realized what I was doing. I narrowed my eyes at her and she looked away, refusing to meet my gaze.

"Henry —"

"No!" he bellowed. "It's too much of a risk for you and the baby. I won't allow it."

I recoiled. "You won't *allow* it? You're not my master, you know."

He closed in, his tired but burning gaze piercing my skin. "No, but I am your husband, and the father of that baby. I will not put you in harm's way, Dianna. Not again. Not ever!"

"Then what will you have me do? Wait around here while you ride off and..." I didn't want to say it. I didn't want to accuse him of something he hadn't even done. But I knew how desperately Henry wished to end my sister's life with his own hands. Could I trust him not to? "I mean, look at you, Henry. You're in no position to be traveling anywhere but back to bed."

Henry stiffened, trying to mask the pain I knew very well he was in. "I'm fine. Shall we discuss this in private?"

I didn't respond, but when he moved aside and invited me to join him outside the dining hall, I followed. I could feel his anger emanating through his skin and wavering in the air around him as he walked a foot ahead. But his labored breaths and the way he favored his good, unburnt arm worried me to no end. I may not be fit to be traveling in the midst on Winter, but neither was Henry.

Once we were inside the adjacent room, a small area that appeared to be used for storing fancy dishes, Henry closed the door behind him and let out a huff of air.

"Henry, you're in no shape to be jumping on a horse in this weather," I said and crossed my arms tightly.

He looked at me, the anger on his face melting away to be replaced with worry. He came toward me and slipped a hand over my ever-growing stomach then took my face in the other. Our eyes, both glistening with concern for the other, searched back and forth.

"I'm a better fit than you," he replied. "There's a doctor here, Dianna. And with the few fainting spells you've had..."

I knew he was right. But I just couldn't bear the thought of Henry facing off with my sister and then losing. And on the opposite end of my mind, I couldn't help but think he'd do it. He'd kill her. And everything I've done would have been for nothing. I could have easily wished her dead and saved the blood on his hands. But that's not what I wanted. She didn't deserve to get off that easy.

"I just..." words escaped me as he brought our faces closer and the warmth of his breath tickled my skin. His mouth, slightly gaped and inviting, lured me in. Weak, I kissed his lips once. Quick and simple, before pulling away. "What will you do when you find her?"

His brow creased in confusion. "What do you mean? I'll bring her back —" Henry pulled back with realization and nodded slowly. "Ah, I see. You fear I'll take her life."

My shoulders shrugged helplessly. "I mean, it's what you've always wanted, isn't it? I know that. And I'm taking that revenge, that closure, away from you."

He held me again, the tip of his thumb brushing under my eye. "Dianna, I had no idea what I truly wanted until you came into my life. Darkness, vengeance, bitterness…. these were what became of me for so many years. I didn't know there was…more. I didn't know there was you."

He kissed me, his soft bottom lip brushing upward to engulf my mouth and steal the breath right from my lungs. When he pulled away, a smile spread wide. "I vowed to respect your wishes. I will not take your sister's life. I will seize Maria and bring her back to you. Alive. I swear it."

I could only muster a nod before leaning my head against his good shoulder.

"I'll shall return in two days," he said quietly. "Lottie will stay behind and watch out for you and the baby. Gus and Finn will be by my side. No harm will come to me, Dianna."

"Okay," I replied, just barely above a whisper. This was it. The moment we'd been waiting for. Months of sailing and nearly losing our lives time and time again…the end of it all was in our grasp. I just wish I felt better about it. I wish my heart and my mind would agree for once. But I just couldn't shake the feeling that something loomed in the darkness ahead. Waiting for us to blink and take it all away.

***

Exhausted from worry, I sat and stared out the carriage window and watched as the deadened winter trees passed us by. Silence filled the small space that early morning as we bound for the little farmhouse just outside the city where Charlie has grown up. I'd been promising to take him home to see his dying mother for so long and, with Henry and the men gone and some free time on my hands, I figured it was just a good a time than any. I couldn't sit around idly at The Siren's Call, waiting for Henry to return. So, after convincing Lottie that I was fine enough to travel by coach for a few hours, she agreed to accompany us to Charlie's home. I stole my gaze from the hypnotizing winter landscape that rushed by and smiled at Charlie who sat quietly by my side.

"Are you excited to go home?" I asked him.

He nodded happily.

"How long has it been?" Lottie asked.

He held up four fingers.

"Four years?" she replied, eyes wide.

She and I exchanged a knowing glance. Four years was a long time to be away from a mother who'd been ill when he left. There was a high chance that we'd be bringing Charlie home to a grave and my heart squeezed in my chest at the thought of his pain. My poor, sweet boy. Even though he was far from it now. I looked at how the softness of his cheeks had somehow hardened to manly cheekbones and how his once-thin and boyish frame had grown and stretched with the muscles of a young man.

I patted his hand. "I'm sure your mother will be over the moon when she sees you."

"What will you tell her of your injury?" Lottie inquired.

Charlie shrugged and pulled out his paper and lead, scribbled something down, and then held it up for us to read.

That I helped save a life.

My eyes glossed over and I hid it with a laugh. "I'll be sure to tell her how brave and foolish you were."

The carriage jostled with a quick turn and Charlie slid forward on the seat to look out the window, eyes wide in wonder and longing. We must have been close. I glanced out and spotted a tiny farmhouse at the end of the dirt road to which we rode on. Cows and horses in the barren winter meadow. A large rickety barn out back.

The house was quaint. A small bungalow with a wide veranda that stretched across the whole front. The carriage came to a stop just as an older man came around from out back, clothes soiled with dirt and a large shovel in his hands. He sat it down on the ground and stood waiting for the carriage to open, a blank look of curiosity on his face. When the door opened, and Charlie stepped out, the man's face brightened and then faltered with a cry as the young man ran to him.

Lottie and I exited the carriage but lingered nearby, so as to give the father and son the chance to reunite without prying eyes. My heart swelled with happiness that at least one parent still remained.

"My boy!" I heard the man say with blubbering lips and his arms wrapped around Charlie tightly. "My boy. You've come home."

They broke free of the intimate embrace and Charlie's father hooked a curious finger inside the white handkerchief he wore around his neck to hide the nasty scars. "What's this?"

Charlie touched his hand and gently pulled it away from the fabric. "Mother?" he croaked.

His father, still unsure about what to think of the glimpse he'd caught of the scar, looked over his son's shoulder at the two women waiting nearby before smiling sadly for his boy. "Mum is...she's inside. Who are your friends?"

Charlie turned and waved us over. My leather boots crunched against the frosty ground as we neared, and I smiled for the man.

"Welcome," he greeted and held out a hand to shake. "I'm Charles Senior. Charlie's father. You'll have to excuse the state of my appearance, we weren't expecting visitors today."

I shook his hand. "Oh, no, please. Don't fuss for us. We're just here to see young Charlie home to see his mother. It's quite the pleasure to meet you, Sir. I'm Dianna White and this is Lottie Roberts."

"It's nice to meet you," he replied. "Thank you for bringing my boy home." He ruffled the hair atop his son's head. "We thought we'd never see him again. Come, let's get you poor things inside and warm up. I'll put some tea on."

We stepped up onto the veranda and followed the man inside the little farmhouse. Tones of warm wood and handmade quilts surrounded from every side and the warmth of a small potbelly stove hugged me tightly as I moved further inside. Charles senior went directly for the tiny white kitchen and put a metal kettle on the stove. Charlie tapped him on the shoulder and raised his eyebrows in question.

It took a moment for his father to follow what his boy wanted, but then replied, "She's in the backroom." He turned to us. "Have a seat, ladies. I'll get your tea ready. Cream and sugar?"

"Yes, please," we both replied and took a seat at the small, wooden farm table. I was surprised when Charlie joined us. But I could see the nervous tremble in the way his fingers wrought together.

I felt wrong encroaching on this very personal moment for Charlie, but he'd insisted on having me with him. Wouldn't have it any other way. I realized now, that he must have been terrified of what he'd find. After so many years away. So, I had to keep reminding myself I was there for him. For support.

"You have a lovely home," Lottie told the man as he brought four mugs of hot water to the table and took a seat with us.

"Thank you." He appeared tired. Not just the kind from a poor night's sleep, but many. Years and years of sleepless nights probably spent caring for his dying wife. His fingers moved without thought to prepare his cup of tea.

"I do what I can when I'm not with Hellen," he continued and then looked to his son. "You should go see her before…"

He couldn't finish the words, couldn't bring himself to say it about the woman he loved. The mother of his child who now sat before him a young man. I stared at the soiled trousers and thick knitted sweater he wore, then remembered the big shovel he dropped to the ground outside. My blood ran cold and my eyes met the man's in understanding. We exchanged a silent nod. Charlie made it home just in time. His mother was dying. Soon. The soil on his father's clothes, grated under his nails, were from the grave he must have been digging out back. Charlie stood from the table and his childlike eyes begged me to come.

"Oh, no, Charlie," I said, "you go. Be with your mother. I shouldn't be –"

But he held out a shaking hand and pleaded. How could I say no to him? How could I let him face it alone? I stood and slipped my fingers into his awaiting hand as he led me to the back room. Slowly, he turned the knob and the door creaked open to reveal a bright and sunny room, a low bed off to the side, and a frail shell of a woman lying in it.

With great difficulty, she raised her heavy head and her mouth gaped open, lips trembling. "Charlie? C-Charlie, my boy?" I could tell she wanted to get up, wanted to stand and hold her boy in her arms, but all she could muster was a set of open hands, beckoning him to come.

He did. Quickly and desperately, Charlie fell into his mother's arms and sobbed into her neck as she held him tightly. I stood in the doorway, unable to look away, trapped and entranced by their love. A mother's love for her child. Something I hadn't witnessed in so many years. It was unlike anything this world could ever conceive. No feeling or entity could match the raw beauty and power of a mother's love for her creation.

Finally, they pulled free of one another and Charlie, eyes swollen and reddened from the tears that poured down his face, took a seat next to her on the bed. It was then that I could get a good look at her. See how frail and sick she truly was. Her beauty was evident, but washed away with pallor skin and dark, sunken eyes. Her lips, grey and cracked, smiled happily for her boy at her side. Then, as if just noticing me there, she glanced up and regarded me.

"And who is this?" she asked and lowered her gaze to my stomach. "Charlie, have you brought home a grandchild for me?"

Charlie laughed and strained to speak with his hoarse voice. "No, Mother. This is Dianna. A friend. She's taken me in. Cared for me."

Her frail, bony hand reached to me and I darted forward to take it, not wanting her to use what little energy she clearly had.

"Thank you," she told me. "For taking care of my son. You don't know what that means to me. I spent years worrying for him. Assured by his letters that he was fine but, still, I worried." She smiled for her boy. "A mother always worries."

"He's a good kid," I told her and then amended quickly. "A good man. Charlie is a fine man. You should be very proud."

"And what's this?" she asked. "Your voice?"

Charlie struggled to find words, to probably tell his mother in a way she wouldn't worry. He cleared his throat but said nothing.

"Uh, he was injured," I spoke up. "He...saw that I was in danger, and stepped in. He saved me from a very bad woman. But it nearly cost him his life. And now...I owe him mine."

Hellen fought back tears and gently pulled down the handkerchief that wrapped around her son's neck, brushing her fragile fingers across the jagged scar there.

"That sounds like my foolish boy," she said. "Always jumping in without thinking. Trying to be the hero. He left to find work when I fell sick," she added and glanced up at me. "Wanted to send money home so his father wouldn't have to worry about the farm. So, he could take care of me." She rubbed his face gingerly and he melted into his mother's touch.

"Yes, like I said, he's a good man." I dropped my gaze to the wooden floor, trying not to think of the way my own mother used to touch my face the same. All this time, I'd tried so hard not to think of her. Tried not to wonder where she was or if she were close by. The woman was everything to me and then she was gone in an instant, pulled from my life like an appendage, leaving me incomplete. For years, I'd blocked out the pain, forgot her touch, and tucked away the love I harbored. And there I was, standing before Charlie and Hellen, suddenly wishing I'd done things differently. That I'd used one of my enchanted pearls to find my mother and not my sister.

"Be a dear and get me some water, would you?" she asked Charlie.

Dutifully, he stood and left the room. I turned to follow but Hellen called to me in a whisper.

"Dianna, please," she croaked weakly, finally letting on just how sick she was. "Do not leave. Tell me. Tell me about Charlie. How he's been." She coughed pitifully. "T-the things he's done."

I shook my head and wrapped the cloak around me tightly. "I, um, I've only had the pleasure of knowing him a few short months. Although, I've come to be very fond of him. Like a little brother. Charlie's a good boy. Spent some time as a deckhand aboard a privateer ship under a good captain." I smiled at the thought of Henry. "Now, he's a deckhand aboard my ship, The Queen."

Her eyes widened as her thin brows lifted. "*Your* ship, you say?"

"Yes," I replied proudly.

"And you're with child?" she inquired.

I nodded. "Nearly five months."

She gawked at my stomach incredulously. "My, you're some size for only five months." When I didn't answer and self-consciously held my belly, Hellen continued with tears in her sick and clouded eyes, "Congratulations. It's a wonderful gift. Cherish it every single day, even when they're not around."

"Thank you." Silence hung between us and I looked anxiously for Charlie's return. Being around the woman, dying or not, it pained me. She reminded me of my own mother so much. *Too* much. I took a few steps toward the door. "I'm, uh, I'm going to go check on your water."

I slipped out and found Charlie, his father, and Lottie standing around in the kitchen, discussing something. They all turned at the sight of me and Charlie appeared happy but anxious.

"What's the matter?" I asked.

Lottie stepped forward. "Charlie's going to stay."

"What?" I looked to him disbelievingly.

Charlie nodded and then strained to speak to me. "Thank you for everything." He paused to swallow hard, showing just how uncomfortable it was to talk. "Please tell Captain Barrett goodbye for me. And to the crew. I'll...I'll miss you all. But I'm home." He looked to his father and then down at the glass of water he held in his hand. "I'm where I should be."

It was the most I'd heard him speak with his new voice since the horrible night in the woods, when Maria's blade sliced through his throat and I watched his small body fall to the ground at my feet. I wasn't ready to let him go then, and I wasn't ready now. But I knew, Charlie was right. He should be with his family. Something I suddenly wanted myself with a deep desperation.

"Of course," I replied and grabbed him, pulling him to me in a tight hug. "God, I love you, Charlie. You'll always have a place aboard my ship. Never forget that." I pressed my face to his ear. "It's your home, too."

I heard him sniffle into my face and I had to pull away, to head for the door before the flood of emotions I felt came crashing down on me like a tidal wave. I kept them at bay until I stopped in the doorway and turned back to them, waiting for Lottie to follow. When I caught a tear stream down Charlie's face, I broke. Everything I'd been bottling up; the fear of my sister, the apprehension of seeing my mother, worry for my unborn child. All of it came toppling down on my shoulders and mixed with the sadness I felt over losing

Charlie. But I had to remember, as Lottie followed me out to the carriage, I wasn't really losing him. I was bringing him home.

And now, it was my turn.

CHAPTER THIRTEEN

When we arrived back at The Siren's Call later that evening, one person less than when we'd left the mansion earlier that day, I felt tired and defeated. I needed some time to be alone with my thoughts and the emotions I'd finally let come to life in my heart. Lottie retreated to her room while I made my way down the winding corridors to the one Henry and I shared.

I entered the empty room, glanced over at the empty bed, and never felt more alone than in that very moment. The day had been long, but not as long as the ride home where I'd sunk into my own mind with thoughts of my mother. I had been pushing away my feelings about her until then, telling myself that I didn't want to see her. That I was better off. Then worse, convincing myself that she wanted nothing to do with me. But now, in this moment, having so much to share, I ached to have my mom.

And I wanted nothing more than to tell Henry about my new revelation.

I walked over to the window and stared out at the sleepy winter landscape, the blinding moon in the black sky, and hugged myself tightly. Trying to contain the emotions that coursed through my body. There was no way I'd sleep. Not tonight. And not without Henry.

I grabbed a small satchel of coins, tightened my fur-collared cloak, and poked my head into the hallway. Looking both ways before sneaking out and gently closing the door behind me. I crept down the hallway toward the front door, thinking I'd take a carriage or a horse myself, but then decided against it for fear of waking someone up. Once outside, I inhaled deeply the crisp night air, admiring the hypnotizing white smoke that exited my body. The evening was clear and free of any snowfall, so I decided to hoof it into the end of town closest to The Siren's Call, the furthest from the docks. I could see the lights of lanterns in the distance and knew I could comfortably walk it in fifteen minutes. I could use the time to clear my head and calm my heart.

As the lights became closer and the sound of a bustling nighttime village touched my ears, my feet sped up. I walked the stone paved streets and admired the towering black buildings, the steaming stacks above houses, and the lovely warm glow of fire lit lanterns hanging from poles. I passed a tavern and peered in through the front window, cloudy with years of neglect, and watched the people inside. Drunken men, card players, and beautiful women to sit on their laps. Cheery music played in the corner and I envied them for the simplicity of their lives. Untouched by the unforgiving magic of the sea or the threat of death looming over their heads.

I turned to leave before I found myself inside and headed down an alley I knew opened up to the streets which would eventually lead to the docks. It was far, the other side of town, but I had all the time in the world on my hands and an empty ship calling my name. But I soon realized...someone else was headed in the same direction.

I was being followed.

The sound of footsteps crunched the frosty ground behind me and quickly multiplied, telling me there was more than one person and my heart beat heavily in my chest. My breath, hot and rapid, filled the air around me and clouded my vision as I glanced over my shoulder at my pursuers. Only thin slivers of moonlight streaming between the buildings caught a glimpse of their moving feet.

"Aye, where ye goin' so late in the night?" one of them drunkenly cooed.

Footsteps sped up.

Another added, "A fine wee thing like ye shouldn't be travellin' down dark alleys." He laughed a gross, gurgled smoker's cackle. "Could be dangerous."

I saw the mouth of the alley up ahead and quickened my pace, but it wasn't enough. The two men pounced forward and grabbed me from behind, yanking me back into the shadows of the alley. I tried to scream but one of their salty hands covered my mouth. I struggled against their hold as my back pressed hard against a stone wall. Knocking the wind from my lungs. One of the fingers slipped into my mouth and I bit down with all my might, sending a fierce growl into the night sky.

Unable to really see my attackers in the pitch-black alley, I took my chance and ran. But, once again, hands were on my body, pulling me back. More aggressive this time.

"Please!" I begged. "I'm pregnant."

A man moved from one side of the narrow space to the other, crossing through a shard of moonlight. His determined face came into view for a split second, but it was long enough to see the malice in his eyes.

"Even better," he replied with a slick tone and closed in as his buddy came from behind, forcing me between them.

I felt his raunchy breath on my face and held back the bile that rose from my stomach, my mind scrambling for what to do. Chastising myself internally when I realized how unprepared I was. No weapon. No way to defend myself. Why didn't I think to take anything?

I brought my knee up, quick and hard, to meet his crotch and sent him reeling back to the ground in a fit of coughing. Before his friend could react, my elbow hauled back and met his nose. The sound of bone-crunching was enough assurance for me. I took off running back toward the entrance, where I knew the tavern was close by and I could hopefully seek help.

But, again, I was too slow. My tired and pregnant body betrayed me. Two sets of hands were on each shoulder, yanking me back into the shadows where I was thrown to the ground like a sack of vegetables. The skin of my bare hands burned as they scraped across the rough stone. I could hear the sound of metal clanking as one of the men removed his belt buckle and I let out another scream.

"Help!"

But a boot came up and smacked my mouth, silencing my cries. Blood rushed to my head and the world around me fell into a muffled pulse.

"Shut up, you bloody whore!" the man told me and then to his friend, "Harry, keep watch, would ya?"

His friend began to walk away, toward the opening of the alley, but was then joined by another set of boots, heavier and clunkier. I heard the wet crunch of a fist meeting face and a body crumpling to the ground just a few feet to my side.

My attacker scrambled to haul his pants back up. "What the –"

More punches were thrown, and the dark alley filled with the sounds two men scrapping. Grunts and groans, painful punches, and then, finally, a second body on the ground. I retreated against the wall, hardly able to catch my breath, and feared what awaited me. A bigger predator had entered the alley and took out my attackers. But what did that mean for me?

Shakily, I strained to see the form in the darkness, only catching a glimpse of the massive man that towered over me. "P-please," I said. "Let me go. I can pay you whatever you want!"

The figure crouched down, catching the moonlight on the back of his head that highlighted his shape like a pale halo. A face hidden in his own shadow. He laughed, low and raspy. "What's the matter? Don't recognize me, sweetness?"

My heart stopped in my chest, unable to believe the voice that graced my ears. It couldn't be...

"Benjamin?" His massive hands reached out in offer and I took them as I hauled myself to my feet where I fell into his arms. I squeezed tightly, fending off the adrenaline shakes. "Oh, my God! I can't believe it's you!"

I felt his body jiggle with a heavy chuckle. "Of course. I promised to find ya, didn't I?"

I erupted into heavy sobs, awash with relief of being saved from the hands of those two men. But, more importantly, the feeling of knowing. Benjamin was there. In front of me and in my arms. Rock solid proof that my wish had worked. In that moment, all the worries I'd been keeping at bay finally released into the wind and I felt as if I could breathe for the very first time.

"It worked," I said and repeated to myself, erupting into a stream of sobs, "It worked. It *worked*."

"Hey now," Benjamin pried me off his chest, "Why the tears? What worked?"

I wiped a trembling hand across the skin under my eyes and laughed. "My wish. It worked."

"Of course it did, sweetness. Why would you think it didn't?"

"I just..." I shook my head, still in awe that my friend was alive and standing before me. "It's not as if the sirens gave me confirmation or anything."

He stood back and held his hands out as he twirled about. "All the proof you need right here. Now," he said and leaned in, so I could make out the slight features of his face, "How about we get out of this alley and go somewhere warm? We've got some catching up to do."

I smiled happily, still unable to believe he was truly there. "I know just the place."

***

I stogged a log inside the tiny fireplace that warmed my captain's quarters and stood, wiping the dirt from my hands. It felt good to be back in my room. Safe from the world. I turned toward my little table, where Benjamin's large frame sat sprawled out, consuming the small chair beneath him. My cheeks hurt from smiling, still unable to believe that my friend was there. Alive and free. But my jaw protested with each word I spoke, reminding me of the boot that had left its mark only a short while ago. I rubbed at the tender bruise I felt forming and shivered at the thought.

"So, this is your rig?" he said as I took a seat across from him.

I glanced around proudly. "Yep, this is The Queen. I've got a small crew, but they're family. It's a good place."

He cocked an eyebrow. "Much better than a bunch'a man-eatin' pirates, I reckon?"

I grabbed a small quilt from the back of the chair and wrapped it around my shoulders, laughing despite the seriousness of what he'd just said. Remembering how close we both came to death at the hands of his insane brother. "Yeah, just a little."

Silence filled the room, packing the holes in between the crackles of the growing fire behind us. My eyes raked Benjamin's body, taking in the sight of him. Still willing my brain to believe he wasn't part of my imagination. He appeared cleaned up, a fresh change of clothes covering his body; brown leather trousers and a loose cream-colored shirt underneath a dark, fur lined trench. His long brown curls still wild and messy around his shoulders.

"How long have you been here?" I asked him. "In town, I mean?"

"Three days," he replied and then stood to grab the kettle of water boiling over the open fire. My eyes followed him back and forth as he prepared a pot of loose tea on the table and sat back down. "I spent most of those finding my way in a world lost to me. Things have...changed."

"Yes, they have." I rubbed my tired face. "Are you okay?"

His thick brow creased over those warm, brown eyes as he regarded me with a look of pain. "I am now."

I realized then, as big of a man Benjamin was, he must have been terrified when he came ashore. And then another thought occurred to me. "Wait, where's your ship?"

He guffawed. "Gone."

"What do you mean *gone*?"

Benjamin groaned a sigh and leaned back, preparing for a long story. "I wasted no time after you left. I had no idea how long it would take you to find the Siren Isles, if at all. But, I knew, if you were successful, I wouldn't have the chance to prepare once the curse began to break. So, I threw my brother overboard, then hauled Pleeman's body ashore. Burned it to ashes. I gathered up my belongings and kept them with me, just in case."

He stopped and lifted a large fabric satchel from his side, bulging with lumps of different shapes and sizes. He looped the long strap over his head and hooked it on the back of the chair before reaching in and pulling out a clay jar and set it on the table.

"What's this?" I asked.

He shrugged. "Pleeman. I gathered his ashes, thinking...if I got out of there, if I, uh, found you...maybe we could –"

I reached across the table and took his hand in mine. "We'll bring him home to his girls."

Benjamin nodded and squeezed my hand, refusing to let go. "After that, I waited. For what, I wasn't sure. The skies to open up? The ship to suddenly set sail? I didn't know what to expect. And the two men who remained despised me for what I did to Abraham. They went mad. I had to tie them up in the brig just to have a moment's peace."

"So, what happened, then? When the curse broke?" I asked, dying to know the details. I'd waited so long for confirmation that my wish worked. That my crew didn't risk their lives at the might of a kraken for nothing.

He shook his head. "I've no idea. It all happened so fast. I was on deck, the sky turned dark and fell silent. Became eerily still. Like a painting. As if....as if it weren't even real to begin with." Benjamin's eyes became lost in the memory. "I felt the ship move, it cracked and groaned from years of being laid up. Like a waking beast. I looked to the horizon, waiting for it to near, but instead...found us plunging downward. The ocean opened up, slowly swallowing us whole. I ran inside Abraham's quarters. Barely made it before the wave came crashing down."

Benjamin let go of my hand then and relaxed back into his chair.

"That was all I remember. I woke up on the beach near the docks here. No ship. No men. But...alive." He smiled, eyes glistening with gratitude. "Thank you."

"No need for thanks," I assured my friend.

He checked the tea and saw that it had steeped. I watched as he poured us two mugs and pushed one across the table for me. I held it up to my face, inhaling the steam, letting it seep into my face and warm my bones.

"So," he said cheerfully and waggled his thick, brown eyebrows, "Tell me everything."

I laughed and settled in to regal him in the tale of The Siren Isles, our great battle with the kraken and how the siren granted me three enchanted pearls. I told him of the wishes, and how I worried they didn't work. He became fascinated with the details of my mission to find my sister and offered to help in any way he could. And then gave me a warm, heartfelt congratulations when I told him of my wedding day. I knew he'd always have a spot for me in his heart, but it wasn't like one would assume. His fondness for me. It went deeper than that. We shared a bond sewn together by the magic of the ocean and the threads of fate. I believed, then, that I was meant to wash ashore on that island. It was written in my destiny to meet Benjamin and break that curse. The man was right where he was supposed to be. In my life, as my friend, and part of my crew of misfit pirates.

For hours, we sat in the warmth of my captain's quarters, going over every single moment and detail since we last parted. Before long, my tired body got the best of me and I couldn't fight off the relentless yawns. Benjamin insisted we get some sleep and he grabbed a pillow and blanket from my bed, tossing it on the floor.

"Well, this looks familiar," he said jokingly as I crawled under the heavy quilts of my comfy bed.

"Tomorrow, before we go to Pleeman's farm, I'll show you to the bunks belowdecks. Get you your own room. You'll be happy here, Benjamin."

"I've no doubt," he replied and stretched out on the floor. "But I'm not sure I can say the same for your husband."

"Henry understands," I told him and fought back another yawn. "I've told him a great deal about you. About us, and what we went through. He hoped for your survival just as I did." And then I added, before my tired head sunk down into my pillow, "Welcome to the family, Benjamin."

CHAPTER FOURTEEN

"**W**here exactly are we going, again?"

Lottie asked and crossed her arms defiantly. She'd been furious when I'd showed up at The Siren's Call earlier that morning with a strange man in tow, after being gone all night with no word of where I went.

"To a farm up North," I reminded her again. "A friend's home."

"This friend," she said, "Pleeman?"

"Yes," I replied and stole a glance out the carriage window.

"The one who is dead?"

At my side, Benjamin grumbled under his breath and turned his attention out the window on his side. He and Lottie weren't exactly off to a great start. He'd bellowed at her to shut up when she went off on me that morning and she'd been giving him the silent side-eye the whole trip.

"Look, Pleeman was a kind old man. He saved my life on that island. And then again aboard the ship." I grasped my cloak at the neck, calming my breath at the memory of Abraham's hands on me. "He...gave his life to save mine. I owe him this."

"We're almost there, sweetness," Benjamin said.

"Stop calling her that!" Lottie cawed.

His eyes widened in annoyance. "I'll call her whatever the damn Hell I please, woman!"

She reached her foot across the carriage and kicked his leg. Benjamin growled and kicked her back. Before an all-out kicking fight ensued, I shifted in my seat to block my two childish friends.

"What the Hell, you guys?" I glanced back and forth, both crossed arms and looked away. "How old are you, again? Four? Jesus. Grow up. Get along." I moved back in my seat as the carriage made a slight turn and caught Lottie's gaze. "You'll have to learn to like one another. Benjamin's part of the crew now."

She balked at my words. "*What*? Does Henry know this?"

I shrugged. "More or less. It's my ship, anyway. I'm the captain and what I say goes. Henry will be happy with whatever choices I make."

Beside me, Benjamin sat up straight and gave Lottie a look of triumph.

She didn't respond, and the carriage finally came to a stop. The door opened and in came a cool gust of light snow, chilling me to the bone. I ached to back in the warmth of my quarters where the little fire burned all night. Benjamin had to pry me from the bed that morning, insisting that my people would be worried. And she had been.

Furiously worried.

Benjamin exited first and then aided me down the couple of steps. Surprisingly, he held a hand out in offer for Lottie, but she refused and jumped from the carriage in defiance. I'd find a way to make them get along eventually.

"This is Pleeman's home?" Lottie asked and gawked at the scene before us. "Are you sure we're in the right place?"

We stood, staring in silence and taking in the sad view of what had obviously once been a thriving home. An overgrown treeline encroached on the dilapidated property; a weathered and leaning house in the distance, a rotten fence stuck up in places through the fallen snow. An old barn, its roof caved in on one side, sat lonely in the meadow. My eyes fell on a wooden sign at the end of the driveway, barely hanging on by a single rusty nail. The words, beaten by time, read *The Whitby's* and a heavy pit dropped to the bottom of my empty stomach. I glance at Benjamin, who also spotted the sign, and we exchanged a sigh.

"No, we're in the right place," I said.

We waded through the few inches of freshly fallen snow, circling the abandoned property. Benjamin went off toward the house, peering in the windows and Lottie took off to the barn. I went out back of the small farmhouse, noting the never-ending stretch of property and admiring the wonderful life Pleeman must have had once upon a time.

But also feeling the crushing sadness of the deserted property, how his family must have packed up and left once they realized he wasn't coming back. A tear escaped and ran down my cheek, turning cold and sticking to the skin there. I spun around and began trekking back toward the house when my foot caught something hard in the snow. With the toe of my boot, I brushed aside some of the dense powder to reveal a small flat stone, raised from the ground, a few jagged letters poking through. My heart caught in my throat as I anxiously wiped away the rest of the white cover.

A headstone.

"Benjamin! Lottie!" I called out. "Over here!"

My two friends rushed over in a huff and stopped by my side where I pointed down. It took a moment, but they realized what it was. Benjamin moaned sadly as Lottie gasped and covered her mouth.

"No," he whispered in the breeze as he knelt down in the snow to further uncover the markings.

The more he shoved aside, the more revealed. Four more stones, each marked with a name. *Gertie*, *Sara*, *Tessie*, *Janny*, and then *Collette*. Pleeman's wife, I assumed. I cried silently as Lottie wrapped one arm around my shoulder, holding me comfortingly. They'd waited. They'd waited for their father and husband to return and he never did. They'd spent their last years on this earth wondering where he'd gone. Probably wondering if he abandoned them. And there he was, trapped aboard a cursed ship, forced to sell his soul until he found a way back to his beloved girls.

Benjamin reached into his satchel and pulled out the clay jar that held Pleeman's ashes, then set it on the ground next to the last grave. Collette's. With his bare, monstrous hands, Benjamin began to hack away at the nearly frozen earth, digging a small and shallow hole. Lottie and I stood by, watching as he popped the cork top of the jar and poured a sprinkle of ashes over each grave before laying the jar down into the hole. He began to sift the loose soil over top when I dropped to my knees at his side. Tears streaming down my face.

"He was brave," I told the stones. "Your father, I promised him I'd tell you how brave he was. He saved my life and it's an act I won't ever take for granted. I'm sorry..." I paused to control the wave of blubbering sobs that poured from my face. "I'm sorry I couldn't bring him home in time."

I leaned into Benjamin and we sat there on the ground, both sobbing as we finished filling the shallow grave with dirt together. My pale, slender finger trembling with sadness as they crossed with his massive ones. When we were done, I let my head fall to his shoulder.

"We did good, sweetness," Benjamin said, his voice cracking under the tears he held back. "Pleeman's home now." I cried as his hand cupped my shoulder and squeezed. "He's home."

I stood to find a stunned Lottie, seemingly unsure of whether to cry or not. She never knew the man we'd just put in the ground. But the effect on my life was evident in my cries and Lottie was my friend. She cared for me, and my pain coursed through her. She never spoke, but wrapped me in a warm embrace, one that lasted until I pulled away.

We walked back to the waiting carriage in silence as the driver nodded in condolence and jumped down to open the door. I glanced back at the old farm once more and said one last goodbye to the man who selflessly saved my life and the family he loved so dearly. Hoping we did right by him. I prayed he was finally at rest and they were all happy somewhere. Together. Benjamin stood by and helped me step in and when he held a hand out for Lottie she accepted it with grace.

Candace Osmond

***

The journey to Pleeman's home up North had been long, so by the time we arrived back at The Siren's Call, night had crept upon us. I was tired and hungry, and missed Henry with every fiber of my body. I itched to have him come back and I realized, on the long, quiet ride home, that he would likely return empty-handed. Benjamin was solid proof that my wishes were working. It just took the universe a while to work out the details. I had asked to find Maria before she killed my mother, and I was willing to bet everything I owned in this world that I was the one who was supposed to find her. Not Henry. Not anyone else. I'd made the wish for myself, and it would be *my* hands that would lay upon her and bring her to justice.

"Where the Christ have you been?" exclaimed Wallace as she barged through the front door to meet us at the carriage. "Dianna, you've been missing the whole time Henry's been gone! What did you expect me to say to him if he returned?"

I was too defeated to deal with this woman. I stopped and looked her square in the face. "Has he returned?"

"Well, no," she said in a flutter.

"Then we have nothing to worry about, do we?" I told her stonily. I motioned to Benjamin, towering over my shoulder. "This is a friend of mine. Benjamin Cook. Would you be so kind as to allow him to stay here with us? I can pay you if it's any trouble."

Wallace shook her head in confusion, her face full of questions. But she bit her tongue and played nice. "Of course," she told me and then sighed, eying Benjamin curiously. "Come, let's get you all fed."

After filling our bellies, I let Wallace show Benjamin to his room and then said goodnight to Lottie. I was wiped. We all were. Drained of all emotions. I dragged my heavy feet across The Siren's Call, down through the marble-paved hallways toward my room. Wishing I could fall into Henry's arms and coast into a deep, comfortable sleep. But none of that mattered once I hit the bed. My eyes managed to stay open long enough for me to toe off my damp boots and haul a blanket up over my bone-weary body.

Before long, I fell into a black void of sleep. Free of emotions or the still imagery of my life. I stood in a dark room, the only sound to be heard was the echoes of my breaths against the empty shell around me. Strangely, it felt good. Being alone. I had no one to worry about. No deaths to mourn. No ghosts to chase. With eyes contently closed, I inhaled the cold air that filled the void and breathed a sigh of relief. Suddenly, a voice sounded in the distance and reverberated through the space around me.

"Diannaaa…."

I spun around, turning every which way, unable to tell what was up or down. Trying to pinpoint the source of the familiar tone that touched the center of my heart. My mother's voice.

"Dianna, baby," the voice called again. "Come here. I'm right herrreee."

"Where?!" I called out in desperation and began walking in the direction of its origin.

It spoke, louder this time, "Right here. I've always been right here..."

"Where? I can't find you!" I cried. "Mom!"

Then, two hands abruptly took me by the shoulders and shook my body, pulling me from my dream world. I gasped for air, as if I'd been holding my breath the whole time and blinked away the remnants of sleep from my eyes. My bedroom slowly coming into focus and the hands still tight on my upper arms.

"Dianna," Henry spoke. "Where are you going? What's wrong?"

Disoriented, I glanced around and realized I must have gotten out of bed and was bound for the door. I...was sleepwalking? Shakily, I let out a trembling exhale and looked to him. My pirate king. How I missed him so. He smelled like cold winter air mixed with the dewy sweat that stuck to his skin. His very presence calming me from the nightmare that still vibrated over the surface of my skin.

"You're back," I noted and leaned against his chest. He winced. "Oh, sorry! I forgot. Here, you probably need new dressings. Sit down." I rubbed at my sleepy eyes.

Before I could pull away, Henry hooked his fingers in mine and yanked me back, taking my face in his hand and covering my mouth with his. I melted into the kiss, warm and engulfing. Like coming home. When he finally broke free, Henry's dark eyes searched mine with concern.

"I missed you," he spoke.

I smiled. "I missed you, too. So much. I never should have let you go off."

Henry sighed, ready to tell me what I already knew, and sat down on the edge of the bed where he removed his shirt. I struck a match and lit the candle next to our bed.

"Yes, and I'm afraid I have bad news," he said solemnly.

I blew the match out and laid it on a plate. "You didn't find her."

"How did you know?"

I shook my head and opened my satchel of goodies, pulling out new bandages and clean cloths to wash his wounds. "I think I must have known all along, just didn't realize it. My wish, it was specific to me. I asked for *me* to find Maria. Not you. Not anyone else."

"Yes, but we still aren't sure your wishes even worked, Dianna." Then he quickly added, "I'm sorry to say. But it's true."

"Well," I replied and soaked a cloth in the basin of room temperature water. It was cool, but it'd have to do. "I have proof that my first wish worked."

"Oh?" he quirked an eyebrow. "How so?"

"Benjamin showed up."

Henry didn't reply, only tried to mask the stunned expression his face held. I went on to tell him everything, from the beginning. About Charlie and his family. And then how Benjamin found me, that we slept aboard The Queen, and how we took Lottie up to Pleeman's farm to bring his ashes home. All the while, I cleaned his healing wounds and dressed new bandages as Henry nodded and listened intently. Seemingly deciding how to feel about Benjamin suddenly being in our lives.

"He's got no one in this world, Henry," I said in the end. "And he's my friend. I want him aboard the ship."

Henry let out a huff of hot air and grabbed hold of my thighs, bringing my body close to his face where it peered up at me from the bed with a fiery intensity. "I'll do whatever you wish, Dianna. Happily. But let it be known that you are *mine*."

I raked my fingers through his long blonde hair, pressing my bosom against his neck as I slid my knees along either side of him. I straddled Henry's waist and could feel his passion for me growing beneath my center. My mouth lowered onto his and placed a single kiss before grinning against it.

"I am yours and you are mine." My tongue flicked out and traced a gentle line across Henry's upper lip.

He growled and dug his fingers deep into my bottom, crushing me against his hips. "God, I want you so bad I can hardly form a thought." The soft bristles of his facial hair rubbed against my neck. "You could command me to do anything and I'd happily be your fateful servant, Dianna."

I threw my head back, letting his mouth devour my bosom as his fingers clawed at the drawstring of my shift. I managed in a breathless reply, "Then take me, Henry. I'm yours."

The man hungrily ripped the thin shift from my body and took me in his consuming embrace where I happily fell into a void of space and time where only the two of us existed.

CHAPTER FIFTEEN

Dreams are a funny thing. They have the ability to wrap you in a world of unreal wonder and then spit you back out into reality, sometimes taking away all recollection of the otherworldly adventure you'd just had.

But sometimes dreams bleed into reality and carry with you. All day. Every day. They're so real that it becomes hard to tell the difference between them and the real world. I often wonder if it's our way of hiding from the harsh realities we face and the stressful lives we live.

All around, meadows of fresh lupins blew in the wind, just like they did by my home in Rocky Harbour, as I stared up a towering stone side. I stood at the bottom of a never-ending staircase that led to the thick clouds above. From them, I could hear her voice again. Calling to me.

"Diannaaa…"

One foot in front of the other, I raced up the stairs, willing myself to go faster but the threads of the dream wouldn't allow it. It felt like forever before I managed to make it past a dozen steps. But her voice beckoned me, and my limbs took on a mind of their own. Reaching for my long-lost mother.

"Mom!" I called to the top. "Wait for me! I'm coming!"

Faster and faster I ran, falling and stumbling as I went. But, still, I persisted.

"Dianna…." her voice danced through the wind, seeming to move further away with every step I took.

I began to panic. "No! Mom, don't go!"

I could see the top, could catch a glimpse of the tall grass that hung down from the cliffside. My feet finally touched the ground and I bent over in a huff, gasping for the air that suddenly escaped my burning lungs. When I stood and glanced around, I found that I was alone. The meadow bare.

"Mom!" I called desperately. "Where are you?"

"Right here," cackled a different voice.

Harsh fingers dug into my shoulders and spun me around. Bringing me face to face with Maria. Her mouth twisted into an evil grin, revealing a few blackened teeth and blood seeping from the corners of her eyes.

"I've always been right here...*sister*."

Her hands, still on me, gripped my upper arms and gave one mighty shove, sending my body flying over the cliff I'd just worked so hard to climb. A guttural scream rang from my chest as I fell endlessly to my death. Just as the ground rushed upwards and my face smacked painlessly against the dirt, I awoke from the dream with a startling cry. Cold sweat covering my skin.

But Maria was still there.

I laid, bound and tied at the wrists, pushed to the floor by my own dead weight. Drool stuck to the side of my face and stuck to the cold floor underneath. Where was I? The room seemed unfamiliar and it felt like hours had passed by since I was last awake. Frozen, my mind struggled to accept the woman laying on floor next to me. Her eyes, full of unhinged rage, bore into mine, just inches away.

I wanted to move. I wanted to scream at the top of my lungs. I opened my mouth to speak, to call for help, but something sharp pressed against my stomach. I glanced down and spotted the tip of a dagger, pinned to the growing mass and my panicked eyes shot back to my sister's face. Her finger, soiled and already bloody, lifted and pressed against her puckered lips.

"Shhh," she hissed. "Don't want to wake Mommy."

I lifted my head and followed her gaze across the room where a still body laid haphazard on a bed. Seemingly lifeless and just thrown there like an old blanket. Long black curls infused with streaks of grey lay in a nest over the person's face. Could it be?

Could it be…my mother?

Maria clicked her tongue, drawing my attention back to her. "You're so difficult," she scolded mockingly. "I've been luring you in for days." Her face flipped to sudden anger and her grimy fingers grabbed hold of my face, forcing me to look her in the eyes even though I already was. "Why are you so stubborn, little sister?"

"M-Maria," I say in a whisper. "You don't have to do this."

"Do what?" she asked, feigning innocence. "Take what is owed to me?"

I shook my head, confused. "What –"

The tip of her dagger pricked the skin of my belly, reminding me it was there.

"This child inside your body." She paused and ran her free hand over my stomach, making my skin crawl. "It will be mine. I'm owed a child for the one *she* wrongfully took from me."

I grit my teeth. "You can't have my baby, Maria."

She shot up and jumped to her feet, flipping the dagger over in her fingers with ninja-like agility before sheathing it at her side. I watched from the floor, unable to sit up with hands bound behind my back, as she paced the room around me. I quickly took stock of my surroundings; dark wood paneling, small fire burning near the back, a grand canopy bed with thick wooden posts. The floor beneath me some sort of stone, cold and pale. Familiar.

Maria strolled over to the fire and stoked it with a metal rod. "You know, I often wondered what made you so special," she said. "Why mother favored you so. Why I was never good enough."

I stole a glance back to the bed, to the body that still laid there unmoving. I willed the person to move, to reveal their face, to give me that confirmation that Maria wasn't fooling me. But I knew, deep down, she wouldn't. This was it. My wish. It finally came full circle and now played out in front of me. I found Maria before she killed my mother. With only moments to spare.

I heard her leather boots clomp against the floor as she came back and let out a loud moan as my body suddenly pulled upright from the floor by my tethered hands, the force pulling at the sensitive skin there. Straining the joints of my shoulders. She pushed me up against a bedpost and yanked my arms up high above my head.

"No!" I cried and attempted to pull away when I realized she was tying them to the canopy.

Maria punched me square in the jaw, sending my head spinning as blood pooled in my mouth. Maria's face twisted with a sick smile as she delighted in the crimson that dripped from my lips.

"What do you think it is?" she asked me, and when I didn't answer, continued, "What makes you so much better? We share the same blood. Do we not?" Her dagger scraped the skin of my face as she dragged it downward, stinging as it trailed across my neck and chest. "Maybe...you taste different."

Her eyes lit up with devilish delight as her tongue lapped the blood from my chin in one big, disgusting lick. She stared at me as the blood swished around in her mouth and I flinched nervously when she spat it all back in my face.

"Taste the same to me." She gave me a shove as she back away, heading back toward the fireplace and grabbing hold of the metal rod. Its tip glowing with a fiery orange.

My eyes widened in horror. "Maria! No, please, I'll give you anything else. Just please don't hurt us!"

Her head tilted to one side. "Oh, I have a whole lot more than a bit of hurt in mind for the likes of you, little sister." She came across the room, hot poker in hand and held its flaming tip in front of my face, grinning at my discomfort. "But you'll come later. For now, I want to play with mother."

I craned my neck and twist around to see her sweep the hair from the unconscious woman's face, revealing the familiar features of a person I'd once known. A person I'd once loved. Still loved.

"M-Mom! Wake up!" I called. But she didn't stir. Tears began to stream down my face, mixing with the blood there.

Maria let out a quiet cackle of laughter as she slowly pressed the hot poker to our mother's face. The smell of burning flesh quickly filling the air between us. The pain rose her from her unconscious state and she shot up with a piercing scream.

"What...what's going on?" She reached up to touch the burnt skin of her cheek and winced. "Where am I?" my mother cried as she looked around, disoriented and in pain. Shakily, she assessed the fresh wound just burned into her skin and let out a silent cry as her eyes scanned the room and then landed on me. A sense of recognition in her gaze. "Dianna?"

I nodded, barely holding the tears at bay.

She lit up, despite the serious pain she must have been suffering, and reached for me. "Dianna!"

But before her hand could touch me, Maria's red-hot poker jabbed into Mom's arm. Another scream filled the room and she fell back onto the bed in a fit of painful cries. It killed me to watch her hurt, to see the inflictions Maria forced upon her, unable to do anything about it.

"Mom!" I strained against my ties.

"The heartfelt reunion will have to wait," Maria said angrily. "I've got plans for you both."

"Maria, please!" Mom begged. "Let Dianna go, and I'll tell you whatever you want. I'll do whatever you ask."

"You've been denying me long enough, Mother! I've been plaguing you for days. You will tell me whatever I wish to know, and you'll do it *now*. In front of *her*," Maria replied and pointed the hot poker in my face. "I want my sister to hear you say the words. Why you hated me so."

"I didn't hate you, Maria, you know that!"

"Lies! You tried to have me killed!"

"I tried to have you *stopped*," Mom corrected, her eyes, just like mine, full of pleading tears. "You're my child. I could never hurt you. But you were a danger to so many. You did so much wrong. It was my responsibility to put a stop to it. If I had known..."

Maria guffawed. "Yet, you couldn't even do it yourself. You got the bloody witch and a pirate to do your dirty work and then stole my child!"

"I gave your son the life he deserves. With a family who will raise him with love."

As my mother spoke, each word filled my ears and wrapped around my heart. I stared at her in awe, unable to believe she was there. Alive. Just a few feet away. I could reach out and touch her, if I had my hands free. It killed me to not fall into her embrace and, as I caught her glistening stare, I knew she felt the same. She ached to grab hold of me and we exchanged a silent *I love you.*

"A better life with those God damn witches? How are they any better than me?"

Mom spoke as calmly as she could. "Maria, you know the answer to that."

My deranged sister began smacking a fist against her own head and paced the floor between us.

"Maria," Mom said, still holding on to the calm tone despite being scorched by the child she pleaded with, "Just let Dianna go."

"No!" my sister screamed in anger. "Tell me why. Tell me how I came to be this way. Why you couldn't love me!"

"I tried!" Mom replied, breaking. "I tried so hard to love you. With every fiber of my being. When Martha pulled me back to the past, stole me from my family in the future, I grieved myself sick. I wished for death."

My throat ran dry as I gawked at my mother, telling her story, saying words I never knew. Giving me a whole new image of how she departed from my life. I'd thought she'd drowned at sea for so long, then,

252

discovered that she'd in fact lived and fled back to her own time. I'd thought she'd abandoned me and dad. But now... to find out that she was taken from me...

Mom's face paled as her eyes spilled over with tears, mouth gaping helplessly. "I-I had no idea," she said to me. "When you were growing up. The things I collected. The research I'd done. I became obsessed with finding out who this mysterious Cobham was. She hadn't existed in my time..."

My stomach dropped as the tightness in my throat squeezed further. "Because she hadn't existed," I said mostly to myself. "Maria, she...you didn't give birth to her until you went back. But that would mean —"

Mom nodded solemnly. "I was meant to meet your father. It was part of my destiny to have you, Dianna. This —" she craned her face around the room, "is all meant to happen in some form or another. Time doesn't exist like we all believe it does. It's a mess of paths, intertwined and striving to exist all at once."

I stared in awe at the woman speaking, how she verified my suspicions about the world. About time and how much fate had played into my life. Dictated every detail and steered me to where I now stood. Details, they're all irrelevant. It's the bonding of souls that tie us together. Dragging us through the murky sands of time.

"Enough!" Maria screamed at us. She neared my mother and held the tip of a dagger to her nose. "I don't care for those parts. You *know* what I want!"

Mom inhaled deeply. "I thought the only thing that could repair the hole in my heart was another child," she continued, glaring at Maria. "I summoned a siren and begged for a baby. Offered anything in return. Even my own soul. The creature asked for a favor, one she could call upon at any time." She paused and shook her head, lost in the memory. "A fool I was. I accepted. I would have given anything, and the siren knew it. Before long, I was with child."

Maria's clunky leather boots paced the floor as her long black jacket fanned behind her.

"So, what happened after that?" I asked. Mom smiled at the sound of my voice speaking to her but then yelped as Maria touched the hot poker to my arm, eliciting a scream from me as it burned through my shift.

"I will ask the questions!" she spat in my ear. She turned to our mother, pointing the burning rod directly in her face. Her eyes wild. "So, I am not born of this earth?"

"No," Mom said apologetically. Her aging, but still beautiful, face turning down into a frown. "You're not. You were conceived by the magic of the sea and grown inside my body. How do you think you came to possess the ability to manipulate a siren's call?"

My stomach toiled at my mother's words. A siren's call? A mythical lure? Had Maria truly been calling to me this whole time? Coaxing me to witness my mother's death and possibly face my own. I had to get free. My mind kicked into overdrive and focused on wiggling my hands free of the ties that bound me to the canopy above my head. The ropes weren't as tight as Maria had probably intended and I felt them loosen with every slight move I made. I did it slowly, carefully. Determined not to call my deranged sister's attention to it. A long sword hung on the wall, the fire glistening against its blade, inviting me to reach out and take it. If I could just break free and lunge for the weapon, I had every confidence I could take my sister down.

But could I save my mother in time?

Maria, seeming to fight with Mom's words, back away, shaking her head and beating a closed fist against it. Mumbling *no, no, no* under her breath. Mom inched forward on the bed, discreetly, closing the space between us.

"You were a beautiful baby," mom continued. "Happy, cheerful. You filled my life with love and joy, helped my heart heal from the pain of losing Dianna and Arthur. But the sirens waited until I was at the peak of my happiness to collect the favor. They asked me to sail out to sea, to a hidden island, and bring back a stolen gem from a cursed ship. They said I may not come back alive, but that my task was to try. I-I couldn't...I couldn't leave you. Not knowing that there was a high chance I could die and leave you an orphan. So..."

I couldn't believe my ears and my brain raced to click all the pieces in place. Mom's task...it was The Black Soul. The siren's heart. She was supposed to get it back and break the curse. But, clearly, she hadn't. Because that perilous mission had been thrust upon me. My mother's cowardice had inexplicably altered my own fate and put me on the path to finish what she couldn't do.

"So, you didn't go," I finished for her.

Mom hung her head in shame. "No, I didn't." She looked up, begging for Maria to look her way. "And the sirens cursed you to punish me. They took your soul and filled you with darkness."

Maria paced the room in front of the fireplace, furthest away from us. Muttering things under her breath and stomping madly as she did. I watched in horror as my sister became even more unhinged than she already was, and I quickened my attempt at releasing my wrists from the ropes. I could almost slip one hand out, if I really pulled hard enough. But that wouldn't be any good and Maria would notice. I had to get both free at the same time.

Just then, Maria stopped pacing and threw her head back in a mad cackle of laughter as she bound back toward us. My blood ran cold. But she disregarded me altogether and went straight for Mom. She hauled her from the bed and tossed her to the floor before reaching into her jacket pocket and pulling out a tiny object. No bigger than a piece of jewelry. My eyes narrowed to see what it was. A ring. A familiar ring. A silver band, white stone like a diamond or quartz. Far too modern for this era.

Maria spun around and looked at me. "You know, it was damn near impossible to find a witch who'd removed herself from the circle. I thought I'd never find one, in fact." She held the ring up, catching it in the firelight. "But did. Right here in Southampton. It took some convincing, but the stupid seamstress finally bent to my will."

Seamstress? I thought as I looked at the ring again, trying to remember where I'd seen it before. My mind just couldn't place it, the memory was just too old. But, when I peered down at the floor and saw the fear and disbelief in my mother's eyes, I suddenly recalled just where I'd seen it.

On her finger.

It was the wedding ring my father had given to my mom so many years ago. I'd admired it as a little girl. And, now, Maria had a witch... "Madam Guthrie?" I asked her.

"Oh, you know the old bag, do you?" my sister said. "Stubborn woman, she was. Claimed to have given up the practice of her people's magic. But she did just fine."

Maria twirled the ring in her fingers before reaching for the dagger sheathed at her side. It slipped out of his scabbard with a shrill sound. My wrists were nearly free. One good yank and they'd both come loose. I just had to wait for the right moment.

"Now it's time to finish this," Maria told us and bent down to the floor next to our mother.

Before I could make sense of what she was doing, the sound of flesh squishing from the pressure of a blade and the wetness of blood sticking to it filled my ears. Mom let out a guttural cry and curled into the fetal position on the floor behind my sister's crouched figure. When Maria moved aside, I could see that she had stabbed our mother in the stomach. Blood seeped through her white shirt faster than I could comprehend and the color quickly drained from her agonized face.

"No!" I yelled. "Why? You don't have to do this!"

The bloody blade pointed to me. "Yes, I do," Maria said with all assurance. Then she placed the ring on the floor next to Mom and forced Mom's fingers to curl around the thick hilt of the dagger. "And I'll do this, as well."

It all happened so fast. If I had realized a second sooner, perhaps I could have stopped it. But I watched, unable to move as Maria lifted our mother's hand and brought it down in one swift, hard thrust. Crushing the stone of the ring. A blinding light shot out from the impact and threw Maria back several feet.

I took that as my chance.

Tearing my raw skin, I yanked as hard as I could and broke free of my ties. I dove for the floor, for my mother, but it was too late. The light had grown, opened up the threads of time and sucked her body into oblivion. Just like I had done not so long ago.

"No!" I screamed, my throat ripping raw from the cries. "Mom!" My fingers clawed at the marble floor, but it was no use. She was gone. All that remained was a pool of her blood.

From behind, I heard Maria scramble to her feet and my sense kicked into overdrive. I had to protect my baby. I had to get out of there. I lunged for the sword that hung on the wall and yanked it from the small hooks that held it there. In the nick of time, I swung around and met my blade with hers in a loud, piercing screech. The sensation of the impact reverberating up through my tired arms. Slack from lack of blood flow.

But I persisted.

I fought with everything I had, meeting her sword with every swing as I backed away toward the door.

"I don't know why I tried to save you," I told my sister. "I should have just wished you dead! You're a monster not fit for this world."

"Like it or not, little one, I'm the only family you've got left!"

Her sword advanced but I pushed back, giving two quick swipes and catching the skin of her cheek. She recoiled, giving me that split-second window I needed to reach for the doorknob. I gave it a twist and flung the door open before running out into the hall. Stunned, I glanced around at the massive paintings and gaudy décor, recognizing it and placing the cold marble floor from the room I just left. Maria followed me out, swinging her blade causally at her side, delighting in my realization.

"Clever, no?" she said. "I was right here under your nose the entire time. Roselynn Wallace was supposed to bring you to me, but she failed." Maria spit on the floor. "She tried and tried to get you to stay put long enough for my call to work. Even burnt down that tavern to force you here. Still, she failed. Worthless bitch. I should have killed that man of hers and been done with it."

Oh, my God. I was still in The Siren's Call. What part of the massive mansion, I'd no idea. But I had to call for help. I had to try. I sucked in a deep breath and screamed at the top of my lungs, "Henryyy!"

Maria erupted into a fit of crazed laughter. "He won't hear you." Her dark eyebrow cocked to on side as her sword arm tightened and raised the blade. "Not in time, anyway."

She advanced quickly, savagely, hardly giving me a chance to deflect. But I kept up, bringing my blade to her time after time after time. Until my arm began to tire even more than it already was and I could feel the ache in my bones. My limbs turned to jelly, and I couldn't lift my sword from the floor.

No one was coming, I realized and then fell to my knees as I finally faltered. Too tired to lift my sword once more. Maria sauntered over to stand in front of me as tears streamed down my face. I said a silent goodbye to my baby, to Henry, and my friends who slept soundly somewhere in that very building.

I'm sorry, I thought. I'm sorry I couldn't beat her.

I heard her blade raise in the air and I glanced up defiantly. I wanted to stare her in the eye when she took my life in hopes that the light draining from my face would haunt her for the rest of her miserable life. However long that may be.

Her mouth twisted to the side, ready, hungry for my blood. I braced for the blow but gasped as her body jerked forward, and a blade burst through her chest, spraying hot blood onto my face. Trembling, I scampered backward, away from the swords, away from the collapsing body of my sister. She craned her neck and twisted her body to reveal the person who so boldly took her life.

"Henry!" I cried out, the relief flooding through my voice. My eyes were on him as he stepped over Maria's lifeless corpse on the floor and dove for me. My body, shaking from adrenaline, fit inside his embrace and he rocked me back and forth.

"Shhh," he hummed in my ear. "It's okay. It's over. It's all over."

I knew he was right, but I let Henry hold me tight as he continued to whisper the words. Again and again. Waiting until it finally rang true in my mind and I could accept that it really was. It was all over.

Maria Cobham was dead.

***

We stood on the cliffs on Southampton, looking out over the docks and the bustling early morning traffic that busied about. We'd gathered there quickly, the whole crew with Henry and I. After he'd pried me from the floor, covered in my sister's blood, we'd emerged to find that the sun had come up and that we had a serious decision to make. One that had to be made quickly. I'd gathered my things and called the crew outside and told them what happened.

"I still can't believe that Wallace had a part in this," Lottie said.

"Don't blame her," I told them all. "Maria was blackmailing her. Roselyn didn't have a choice. Tell her that I know that now, okay?" I motioned to Lottie who was fighting back tears. "Tell her?"

She nodded.

Finn stepped forward. "Christ, do ye have to go so soon?"

I flung myself into his giant arms and he placed a kiss atop my head as I heard a slight sniffle come from his nose. "Yes, if Mom's ring was from the future —" I choked back tears. "Time isn't really on our side right now."

The big Scot chuckled and wiped away a fallen tear. "'Tis never on our side, Lassie."

"I know," I told him. "And I'm sorry. I'm going to miss you so much. You have no idea." I glanced around at the crew before me. Finn, Gus, Lottie, and Benjamin. Seamus and John had gone into town the night before, but they'll understand, once Gus told them.

"Augustus," Henry spoke and held out a hand. Gus accepted it proudly. "You're the captain of The Queen now. She's yours. Treat her well."

"Aye, aye, captain,' Gus replied, holding his head high and then glancing to Lottie. "We all will."

Lottie grabbed hold, pressing me against her in a crushing embrace. "Don't forget me, alright?" she said in my ear.

"I could never," I whispered back to her. "I love you, Lottie."

We broke free of our embrace and I returned to Henry's side. "Are you sure you'll all be alright to sail back to Newfoundland?"

"Aye," Finn churred. "We'll be just fine. I reckon we'll wait out the winter here. Git on Wallace's nerves fer a while. She owes us as much."

"You'll be happy aboard The Queen," I said to Benjamin. "I promise. They'll be your family."

He nodded sadly and pursed his lips. "I know, sweetness. I know." He nudged the snow on the ground with the toe of his boot, unsure of how to really say goodbye. I knew the feeling. "Are...are you sure you can't wait just a little longer? I mean…I just got here." Benjamin grinned sadly.

I pulled the man into a desperate hold. "I wish there were more time," I said in his ear. "But I have to go now if I have any chance at all."

Pulled away, reluctantly, aching with every inch I put between myself and my friends. I had to keep reminding myself that I was leaving them with everything they could ever need. They'd be alright without me. Without us.

I sighed. It was time to go, but I couldn't bring myself to leave them. To turn my back to the people I'd come to love. Come to call family. But I had to remind myself that they had each other, the ship, and enough treasure to last ten lifetimes.

"Go!" Finn bellowed, making the hard choice for me. "Git on outta here!"

I looked at Henry and he secured his grip around my fingers. We ran off down the path that led to the bottom of the cliff, toward the water. When we reached the bottom, the brave man stopped and turned to face me. His dark eyes gleaming down with a mix of joy and uncertainty flashing in their reflection.

"Are you sure?" he asked me.

"Of course, " I told him. "I know what to expect. I know where we're going. But…are you sure? Are *you* ready?"

Henry held my face in his hands and covered my mouth with his. The warmth of his lips soothing my bones and filling my soul with love. My pirate king. My everything. When he pulled away, he smiled.

"I am always sure when I'm with you," he said to me. "And, I'd say it's about time we have our happy ending, don't you? We deserve as much."

I pulled the final pearl from my jacket pocket and pinched it between my fingers as my heart beat wildly. I tossed it in the shallow ocean and squeezed Henry's hand.

"Yeah, it's about time."

EPILOGUE

I sat on the front porch, newly painted a fresh white, and wrote in my brown leather journal, as I often did on days like this. Filling it with tales of my adventures as they rushed back like recent memories.

The sun began to set over the harbor and cast a ripple of purple and orange on the sparkling water. I smiled at the sight of the sunlight touching the pale reflection of the moon. With closed eyes I held the nearly full book to my chest, dreaming of a time when I ruled the sea with my friends. Recalling their faces and the warmth of their love.

Behind me, footsteps sounded across the wide porch and sidled up next to me. I opened my eyes and smiled at my Henry. My husband. My soulmate. He'd adjusted to life in Rocky Harbour just as I'd always imagined. As if he belonged there. He still wore the ratty old sweater that aunt Mary had knitted for him before she passed, and told me he'd just come back from fishing in the harbor.

He smiled, kissed my forehead, and handed me a mug of steaming tea.

"Thanks," I said and craned my neck, reaching for another kiss. On the lips this time. He laughed and touched his warm mouth to mine. "Catch anything today?"

"Yes," Henry replied and raked his fingers through his blonde hair. He kept it shorter now, wanting to fit in with the new world. But it still flopped down around his ears and I adored it to no end. "Five. They're in the sink." He took a sip of tea. "Where's the kids?"

Just then, as if hearing their father from across the meadow, two blonde heads of curls came running through the tall grass toward us.

"Daddy!" they called out in unison and then clobbered on top of Henry after they scampered up the stairs. Henry took them in both arms and kissed their little heads. "You stink like fish!"

They both jumped up and ran as Henry playfully chased them with his fishy fingers, their little screams of joy warming my heart. Arthur and Audrey. My whole world on one porch. I sometimes wondered if we made the right decision by coming back to the future, back to Rocky Harbour. But at times like this, I knew it with the deepest certainty. We were safe. We were loved. We were happy.

A car came rolling down the long gravel driveway and stopped just a few feet from the porch. I stood and smiled as the driver's side door creaked open and a woman stepped out. She strolled toward the house, cane in hand. The kids spotted the visitor and turned their wildness on her.

"Grandma!"

They ran for Mom and wrapped their tiny arms around both her legs.

"Hi, babies," she greeted them and then bent down to get a better hug from each.

I laughed as she pulled out a small container of cookies from her jacket. They grabbed it like a couple of vultures and ran off inside the house.

"Oops, hope I'm not ruining their supper," she said in a very grandma-like way. Knowing very well she was. "Am I late?"

"No, Mom," I replied and took her hand as she climbed the few stairs to the porch. The stab wound forever impairing the use of her right side. A constant reminder of that horrible night. "Henry just brought the fish in. I'm tossing them on the grill in a second."

She looked at me with pride and heaved a happy sigh. "God, I love you."

I smiled and took her by the hand. "I know. I love you, too, Mom."

***

Later that night, after Henry got the kids to bed and Mom had gone home to the house Aunt Mary had left her, I took a stroll down by the water, as I often did. It was my way of being close to them. Our crew and friends that we'd left behind. The siren had once told me that the ocean was somehow connected throughout time, always existing. Like a constant. I bent down and touched my fingers to the water. The same water that Lottie, Finn, Gus, and Benjamin sailed on, and I felt them.

"I miss you guys," I whispered to the night sky. "Please know what we're safe. We're happy. And I hope you are, too."

Ripples formed on the calm surface and vibrated toward me, growing more rapid as something bobbed in its center. I backed away, knowing very well what it was.

"Show yourself," I said to the sea creature.

The center of the ripples raised higher until the shape of a head, formed of water, appeared. Clear eyes blinking up at me.

"Hello, Dianna Cobham," spoke the music box voice.

"I'm Dianna White, now," I corrected.

"Regardless of your name, who you are remains the same," the siren replied.

"What do you want?"

She raised from the water completely and shimmered as her clear body took shape, scales of shells and hair of kelp taking on the vibrant colors of the sea. Her toothy mouth turned up in a grin. "Don't you know by now?" she said. "You made a deal. To go back in time in exchange for a favor."

My throat tightened, and I swallowed hard against it. The siren advanced slowly, grinning wide.

"And I've come to collect."

THE END

Candace Osmond

ABOUT THE AUTHOR

Published author and freelance writer/editor, Candace
Osmond was born in North York, ON.
She published her first book by the age of 25, the first
installment in a Paranormal Romance Trilogy to which two
others were published with it. The Iron World Series.
Candace is also one of the creative writers for sssh.com, an
acclaimed Erotic Romance website for women which has
been featured on NBC Nightline and a number of other
large platforms like Cosmo. Her most recent project is a
screen play that received a nomination for an AVN Award.
Now residing in a small town in Newfoundland with her
husband and two kids, Candace writes full time developing
articles for just about every niche, more novels, and a
hoard of short stories.

**Connect with Candace online! She LOVES to hear
from readers! *www.AuthorCandaceOsmond.com***

GET MORE FROM
AUTHOR CANDACE OSMOND!

Candace's main genre is Fantasy Romance, but she often delves into other worlds. check out some of her bestsellers in other genres!

The Iron World Series
Three mythical races. Decades of ancient war. And the love of one girl to save them all.

The Donor
Step outside of Fantasy Romance as Candace takes on the world of Scifi Romantic Suspense with The Donor. Orphan Black meets Fringe in this gripping story.

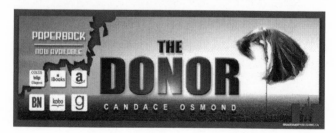

Killer Me

Candace's passion project, Killer Me is a Psychological Thriller with an Alice in Wonderland twist. Alice Teller is about to fall down the rabbit hole where her estranged father waits in the shadows, hoping she'll follow in his footsteps…as a serial killer.

Silently into the Night

What would you do if the man you loved was destined to reap your dying mother? That's the choice Rose faces in this gripping Paranormal Contemporary Romance about the grim reaper and his quest to find true love. No matter the cost.

Made in the USA
Columbia, SC
17 September 2019